Dear Diary,

Our mystery baby finally has a name—little Phoebe Marino.

Shana came down to tell me the news. I still say a prayer of thanks that she's come into my life. I hope it's just a matter of time now before her brother, Brett, feels the same pull of family.

Brett—he's a real loner. An I-don't-need-anyone-in-my-life kind of guy. That's probably why he makes such a good P.I.—ready to pick up and leave as soon as a new missing-person case comes up.

And he's good at his job. He's the one who tracked down the baby's mother—Layla Marino—to her isolated mountain cabin.

I don't envy Brett his mission—telling a mother that the child she's loved and nurtured for the past two months is really not hers, and that her own baby is waiting for her in Seattle.

But there might be a bright side to all of this. Since Brett's been snowed in up on that mountain with Layla, Shana senses from his phone calls that he's changed. He's beginning to feel again. To speak from his heart instead of his head.

Sometimes I think things really do happen for a reason. I have faith that both babies will be fine—they have so many people who love them. So what if, after all these years of pushing people aside, these two loners find love with each other?

Unlikely? Perhaps. But then, I'm always looking for a happy ending.

Till tomorrow,

Alexandra

ISABEL SHARPE

was not born with a pen in her hand like many of her fellow authors. Instead of starting a writing career early in life, she got her B.A. in music from Yale in 1983 and a master's in vocal performance from Boston University in 1990. In 1994 motherhood happily interrupted a fledgling career in fund-raising for which she was vastly unsuited. Searching for something to keep herself stimulated while at home full-time with a demanding infant, she took the plunge into writing romance. Since then she has sold fourteen books to Harlequin—six Harlequin Duets novels, one Harlequin Temptation title, four Harlequin Blaze books and three special projects. Isabel has been a member of Romance Writers of America since 1996. She was a 1998 Golden Heart Finalist and a 2003 RITA® Award finalist in Short Contemporary. Isabel lives in Wisconsin with her two sons and a paunchy cat named Sinbad.

Forrester Square

LEGACIES . LIES . LOVE .

ISABEL SHARPE
SECRET LULLABY

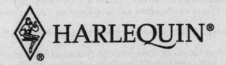

HARLEQUIN®

TORONTO • NEW YORK • LONDON
AMSTERDAM • PARIS • SYDNEY • HAMBURG
STOCKHOLM • ATHENS • TOKYO • MILAN • MADRID
PRAGUE • WARSAW • BUDAPEST • AUCKLAND

HARLEQUIN BOOKS
225 Duncan Mill Road, Don Mills,
Ontario, Canada M3B 3K9

ISBN 0-373-61283-4

SECRET LULLABY

Isabel Sharpe is acknowledged as the author of this work.

Copyright © 2003 by Harlequin Books S.A.

This edition published by arrangement with Harlequin Books S.A.

® and TM are trademarks of the publisher. Trademarks indicated with ® are registered in the United States Patent and Trademark Office, the Canadian Trade Marks Office and in other countries.

Visit us at www.eHarlequin.com

Printed in U.S.A.

Dear Reader,

I generally write light comedy or sensual romps, so this book was a departure and a challenge. Trying to get into the mind and feelings of a woman who shuns society and who is forced to give up a child she's raised as her own was fascinating and often emotionally difficult.

I have to admit, though, I loved giving this determined hermit heroine a hero strong and persistent enough to make her realize how lonely and isolated she really is! Just in time for a happy ending to her story and the whole FORRESTER SQUARE saga.

I hope you enjoy it!

Isabel Sharpe

www.IsabelSharpe.com

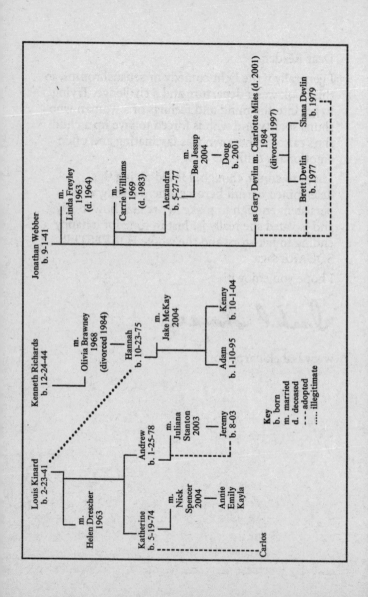

Louis Kinard
b. 2-23-41

Kenneth Richards
b. 12-24-44

Jonathan Webber
b. 9-1-41

m.
Helen Drescher
1963

m.
Olivia Brawney
1968
(divorced 1984)

m.
Linda Freyley
1963
(d. 1964)

m.
Carrie Williams
1969
(d. 1983)

Katherine
b. 5-19-74

Andrew
b. 1-25-78

Hannah
b. 10-23-75

Alexandra
b. 5-27-77

m.
Nick Spencer
2004

m.
Juliana Stanton
2003

m.
Jake McKay
2004

m.
Ben Jessup
2004

Annie Emily Kayla

Jeremy
b. 8-03

Adam
b. 1-10-95

Kenny
b. 10-1-04

Doug
b. 2001

as Gary Devlin m. Charlotte Miles (d. 2001)
1984
(divorced 1997)

Brett Devlin
b. 1977

Shana Devlin
b. 1979

Carlos

Key

b. born
m. married
d. deceased
– – – adopted
.... illegitimate

PROLOGUE

BRUCE LEHR HUNG UP the phone in the kitchen of his new Seattle house and slumped down in a chair, one of the few surfaces in the entire place not covered with boxes.

His fiancée, Anne, took one look at his face, put down the glass she was unwrapping and walked over to him. Kneeling in front of him, she put her hands on his knees. "What is it?"

She said the words quietly, her lovely face anxious but calm. She had enough strength for both of them. He knew that, and he adored her for it.

"Jim's dead. Only a few weeks ago. Car accident. After twenty years I decide to find my brother, and I miss him by only a few weeks."

Anne's face crumpled in sympathy. "Oh, sweetheart, I'm so sorry."

Bruce dragged his hands up to his face and took in a deep breath. His older brother had run away from home twenty years ago at age fifteen. A bad seed, his parents had said. Drugs, violence, bad crowd, you name it. Bruce had been thirteen, entering adolescence, confused, anxious, grief-stricken. He'd done the rest of his growing up without a brother, gone on to college, graduate school and a career in international law. By the time his parents died, he'd become a tunnel-visioned workaholic, cut off from his family and his country.

Until he'd met Anne. In Paris, the city of lovers. He'd fallen madly in love, and the world had immediately opened up to him as a place full of joy and discovery. He'd vowed to live the rest of his life reaching out instead of looking in. And if that made him sound like a sappy freak, tough. Every word was true.

He'd decided to move back home to Seattle, where he was raised, to start his own law practice, to raise a family and to reconnect. Even the startling and devastating news that Anne wouldn't be able to have children had only broadsided them for a while. They'd adopt. Bring children into their warm, loving home who might not have access to one otherwise.

First, though, he'd wanted to find the last living member of his family, his brother, to invite him to be best man at his wedding next week, and to begin rebuilding family ties. The process of tracking Jim down had taken much longer than he'd expected. Finally he'd called the Seattle police and gotten this awful news. A few weeks had robbed him of that one chance to get close to family again.

And given him another.

"Anne." He looked into her sad brown eyes, took her face in his hands and brought her up to nestle on his lap, his heart full to overflowing with the anguish of a missed opportunity and the beautiful hope that he could do something to help heal it all. This wasn't what they had planned, not the timing they'd ever imagined, but in many ways it was the answer to all his dreams.

"Jim died with his wife in the wreck. But, Anne…"

She lifted her head from his shoulder at the husky emotional croak his voice had become.

He smoothed back the soft dark hair from her face. "They had a child."

CHAPTER ONE

BRETT DEVLIN inspected the contents of his refrigerator with mounting disgust. Half-empty jar of jalapeno-stuffed olives, natural peanut butter, skim milk, orange juice, pickles, ketchup, the last of a pot of chili made way, way too long ago, eggs... The peril of being on the road so much—nothing for dinner. He pushed the door closed, jammed his hands on his hips.

He couldn't take another meal at Ida's Good Times Café tonight; he could recite her menu in his sleep— and probably did sometimes. Three things were inevitable down at Ida's, corner of Main and Cherry in Detail, Nebraska: greasy food, strong coffee and remarks about how he needed a woman to take care of him.

Tonight he wanted something different. Some celebration was in order after he'd wrapped up a particularly tough missing child case and returned home today. Against all odds, he'd found the kid alive and well, not doped up or starting a career in delinquency as his hysterical parents were convinced, just sulky and adolescent and feeling misunderstood. A tearful reunion, then Brett passed along the business card of a recommended family therapist and wished them the best of luck.

So Brett felt good. A little restless maybe, but good. This mood always found him when he arrived home between cases. The high of success tempered with edginess and the unsettling certainty of oncoming discontent. He didn't like too much time on his hands. After the first week back, catching up on cleaning and bills, exercising and doing crossword puzzles, he began to starve for action, body and brain.

Too much downtime led to brooding. Over what was, over what could be, over what might have been. A complete waste of energy.

He opened the refrigerator door again, grabbed the eggs and a shriveled half of a green pepper lying forlornly in the produce bin. Garlic, onions, parmesan cheese. Loaf of French bread in the freezer, bottle of beer. Or two. He'd manage. Not quite a celebration, but not so bad, either, and no Ida telling him he needed a woman to take care of him.

Like he needed a hole in the head.

His satellite phone rang. He grabbed for it, feeling the customary mix of anticipation and apprehension. The push and pull between wanting more time to himself and wanting more work. Between not wanting to hear about more evil and needing to put it right.

"Brett, it's Shana. Where are you?"

He rolled his eyes with good humor. His little sister was using her I'm-so-worried voice. Which meant one of two things: he hadn't called recently enough or she was off on another cause. She loved causes. If she ran out of her own causes, she took on other people's just to keep the fun going. "I'm home. What's going on?"

"Oh…nothing much. How are you doing?"

Brett suppressed a grin. "Out with it."

"Out with what?"

He could practically hear her eyelashes batting innocently. "Whose butt needs saving now?"

"I can't call just to see how you are?"

"Yes, you can. But this isn't one of those times. Out with it."

"Well…there is some news."

"Oh, really?" He smiled to temper the sarcasm in his voice.

"It's about Chris."

Brett's smile left him. Chris, Shana's "mystery baby" foster daughter, had been abandoned in a hospital after the woman brought in with her had died as a result of a car accident. Tests showed the woman had given birth—but not to Chris. The infant had been lucky enough to land Shana and her new boyfriend Keith as foster parents while the frantic search to locate her missing and equally mysterious birth mother went on.

"Is she okay?"

"She's fine." Shana's voice softened. "She's wonderful."

"So what's up?" Brett let himself relax and grabbed a well-seasoned omelet pan from the scarred oak cabinet to the right of the sink.

"Jaron and the Seattle P.D. think they've found her birth mother."

"No kidding." He put the pan on the stove and pulled a wooden cutting board closer on the counter. "What's the story on her?"

"They think Chris was switched with another girl at birth—" His sister's voice broke. "Deliberately."

Brett sighed. While he couldn't blame Shana for loving a child that had been in her care, she was letting herself get eaten up unnecessarily. People did things for screwed-up reasons. People were horrible and selfish all over the place. You couldn't let it get to you.

Somehow, even after their messed-up childhood, Shana refused to accept that. Half the time he admired her, the other half he wanted to shake some sense into her.

"Sounds like a bad deal." He extracted a small mixing bowl from the graduated stack on the shelf at eye level and opened the carton of eggs. If he was going to deal with more of "As Shana's World Turns," he needed sustenance.

"Don't you see?" Her voice took on the husky pleading tone that always spelled trouble for Big Brother Brett. "That means that somewhere out there is a mother who doesn't know her two-month-old isn't hers."

Brett cracked three eggs into the bowl and grabbed a fork. "So you think it's a good idea to bust up a perfectly happy family and inflict unbearable trauma on mom and baby, who right now are enjoying life in blissful ignorance?"

"The baby isn't hers."

"Blood isn't what makes a family. We, above all, should know that." He beat the eggs more vigorously than he needed to.

"Oh, please." Shana sighed. "Do we always have to go through your cynical hard-as-nails P.I. act? Can we please, just once, skip to the part where you admit you have a heart and that you're compelled to do what's right as much as I am?"

"I don't believe in going out of my way to take on other people's problems." He put the green pepper half on the cutting board, picked up a chef's knife and went at it. "That's your department."

"Oh?"

"Oh."

She laughed with I'm-gonna-blow-that-one-outta-the-water certainty. "What about the time you helped me look for Whiskers for three days when he got trapped in Mrs. Garfield's barn?"

"That was strictly self-preservation. You were driving me nuts with your whining."

"What about the time you beat up Charley Harrison for picking on Louise Chambers?"

"I owed him one." He dumped a lump of butter and the chopped pepper into the pan, turned on the burner and grabbed an onion. "Convenient excuse. Allowed me to give him what he had coming and look good at the same time."

"Uh-huh. What about the time you took the blame for Ralph Press making rude noises in gym class because you knew he couldn't handle the punishment laps and everyone would laugh at him?"

"Shana…"

"What about the career you picked? What do you do for a living, Brett? You solve other people's problems! Hello? Hello?" A loud tapping noise came over the line. "Is this a bad connection or am I getting through?"

"I don't get involved. It's just my job, not some bleeding-heart crusade." The onions followed the pepper; he gave the pan an expert flip and spilled half of the vegetables onto the burner. "I do it because I'm damn good at it and because I get paid."

"Right. Whatever." He knew without seeing her that she was rolling her eyes.

"Okay, okay. So I'm glad you found Chris's mother. You can switch the babies back. Except for the small matter of the shock and misery they have to go through first, everyone will live happily ever after.'' He scooped up the runaway peppers and onions from the stovetop.

"Well…"

Something in her voice made him freeze, and then wish he hadn't when the retrieved vegetables started burning his hand. "Well, what?"

"We haven't exactly found her."

"I thought you said—"

"Jaron Dorsey—the detective on the case—located her last-known address. After that the trail goes cold."

Brett tossed the peppers and onions back into the pan and pressed his hot palm to the cold tile of his counter. He was starting to have a pretty good idea where this was going. "You wouldn't by any chance be calling me for some reason other than to bring me up to speed on the latest developments, would you?"

"Brett…" His sister pumped even more need into the voice that always undid him, though he'd never let on. "You could not only find the needle in the haystack, but who put it there and why."

He gave the pan another flip, this time neatly catching each leaping vegetable piece on its way down. "I swear, you are getting to be as manipulative as Mom."

She laughed, understanding his grumbling for the frustration release it was. "At least I manipulate to bring people together, not drive them apart."

"I can't imagine Jaron Dorsey would welcome me in on his case. I'm sure there are plenty of cops and/ or P.I.s in Seattle under his jurisdiction who can handle the job." He poured the eggs into the pan and swirled the mixture with a fork.

"Possibly. But this case is personal to me. Jaron doesn't mind if you give it a shot. In fact, he welcomes the help. You're not only the best tracker in the country, but I know you will handle this with the sensitivity it needs, even if you persist in pretending you're a Neanderthal. Chris needs to be back with her birth mother.''

''A mother who has already bonded with the infant she has, who doesn't know it isn't hers. Leave it alone, Shana. It's not for you to play God.''

''But it's not fair to her that—''

''So life isn't fair. When are you going to live enough of it to figure that out?'' His voice came out harsher than he intended and he grimaced. Shana had made it this far in life with her faith in humanity intact. She didn't deserve to be beaten with his cynicism.

''Brett.'' Her voice dropped to a quiet warning. ''There's something else.''

Brett put down the fork. He turned off the stove and put the pan on a cold burner.

''What?''

''Jim Lehr, the husband of the baby-switching couple who died in the car accident? He had a brother, Bruce, who just moved back to the States after living abroad. Bruce Lehr contacted the police when he couldn't find Jim.'' Shana took a long, shaky breath. ''And he desperately wants his niece.''

LAYLA MARINO'S EYES flew open into total darkness. Baby. She lifted up onto one elbow and pushed the hair out of her face, her breasts already responding to her child's cry for food. Instinctively she knew it was earlier than Baby usually awoke. The infant made it to at least five on most mornings.

She scooted closer to the edge of her bed and reached into the tiny crib her father had made out of scrap wood and painted pale yellow. He'd presented it to Layla on her eighth birthday, twenty-one years ago, with Layla's cherished rag doll, Mattie, nestled inside. Even at the time Layla had been amazed that in his usual state of altered consciousness and with his rough, thick harvester's fingers, he could make her something so beautiful. Now it seemed nothing short of a miracle.

Baby settled at the touch of Layla's hands, making Layla marvel for only about the thousandth time at the power of a mother's touch. She brought the warm bundle into bed with her, lay on her side and pulled up her shirt to the chill November morning air, cradling the child in her left arm, offering her breast to the greedy soft mouth with her right. The child latched on and started suckling, expert now at what had seemed so foreign to her in the first week of her life.

Layla covered both of them and smiled as the hormones flooded her, relaxed her to deep peace, idly stroking the soft blond wisps on Baby's head. She'd chosen the name Phoebe for her daughter. Chosen it when she herself was a little girl in California. She could barely remember which school it was where she'd met Phoebe's namesake, which town, which grade, but she'd never forget the moment.

She'd come to school, another day of being one of the "new kids." Worse, one of "those" new kids. The migrant worker kids. She was six, maybe seven. The teacher had gestured toward an empty desk next to one of the most beautiful girls Layla had ever seen. She'd had long blond hair, deep blue eyes, and a perfect pouty mouth, like a doll's. She wore a white dress printed with clumps of black-stemmed, bright red cherries and soft-looking red shoes not stained by dust or dirt.

Layla hadn't been able to stop staring. The girl seemed to represent both the joy of everything Layla could become and the pain of everything she wasn't. Clean pretty clothes and, even more, that fresh, untouched quality. That vision of Phoebe cemented the determination Layla'd always had—that she wouldn't end up like her parents, brains rotted by addictions, lives rotted by blown opportunities, looked down upon by everyone and not even caring. Layla would make a different life for herself and her children.

Of course, perfect little Phoebe had turned out to be the perfect little self-serving brat-monster-from-hell who'd made Layla and everyone else around her envious and miserable. But even that hadn't tarnished the power of that image on another first day in another eventually anonymous school.

She let out a sigh loud enough to startle Baby, who pulled back without breaking suction, eyes wide, arms jerking outward. Layla stroked her and whispered comforting words until Baby closed her eyes once more and settled back into her sucking rhythm.

The problem—and it was a pretty damn huge problem—was that even though she'd put Phoebe Marino on the birth certificate, Layla couldn't bring herself to use the name for this child.

It sounded crazy. It was crazy. She'd told herself so over and over again. If she had anyone to talk to, which of course she didn't, living in a cabin in the middle of the Cascade mountains, no doubt they'd say she was crazy, too. But all her life she'd had a vision of what her children would look like. Two boys and a girl. Colin, Jack and perfect Phoebe.

She'd missed the first sight of the child coming out of her body. She'd lost too much blood, had been slipping in and out of consciousness. She dimly remembered the rush of the final separation, the O.B. shouting, "Meconium," which meant she'd seen fecal matter in the amniotic fluid and Baby's lungs would have to be carefully suctioned by a neonatologist to prevent infection. Layla remembered the sense of loss, after all that work, to have her baby taken away.

After that, things had blurred. There'd been pain, too much bleeding, more shouting, and finally the relief of the general anesthesia abyss. Then the dreams—or were they memories?—of struggling through the birth, of struggling back to consciousness, of her infant daughter, bloody, godawfully misshapen from the tough trip, but beautiful, so achingly beautiful.

Such vivid dreams. To the point that when she'd finally come to and the nurse had handed her this darling little child, Layla had had to bite back the words that jumped to come out: "I'm sorry, this isn't her."

What kind of ungrateful wretch would that have made her after the staff had just saved her life? Mooning after a fantasy child from her dreams?

She gave a humorless chuckle. An enormous, ungrateful wretch. Though she shouldn't beat herself up too badly. She'd read in one of the books she bought in a panic when she found out she was pregnant that not all mothers bond instantly with their children. Not all mothers feel that legendary swell of love and devotion and, more important, connection, right away in the delivery room. On some level that made sense. The little person they handed her was a stranger. Real love grew after two people got to know one another.

The problem was that now, nearly two months later, the sense of distance from the child was still there. Instinctive protectiveness was strong. Affection, tenderness and the urge to nurture were strong. But she'd expected a deeper bond, a sense that they shared so much more than living quarters and routine. The sense that this child came of her flesh and blood and DNA and should therefore be so much a part of her that they operated as a single unit.

Worse, much worse, along with the haunting distance came fear. Fear that her decision to bear the child had been a mistake. Fear that she'd shut herself off from people and emotions for so long that even her own flesh and blood couldn't awaken them. Fear that she simply wasn't able to love, even in the least complicated and most free way that anyone could love.

As much as she was content to live alone in this cabin, her very own stable, wonderful home, sometimes she wished she had more than books and her pediatrician as resources for her questions. She couldn't exactly tell her doctor that she wasn't sure she loved her child enough. Dr. Blotts was a kind man, but he'd just shoot her one of those hawkish looks from under his bushy brows and make a note in his file to keep an eye on the weird mountain woman in case child services needed to get involved.

What Layla needed was a girlfriend who was going through this tough journey of exploration at the same time, or maybe an older woman, since Layla's mom was long gone. Even a pen pal would help. Someone who would understand the overwhelming nature of the job of being a parent. She thought of Karen Packard, her mentor at Sunshine Kids, a program for promising migrant children. Karen had been the closest Layla ever got to a good mother. But Karen had no children of her own.

Baby was almost asleep now; little bursts of sucking interspersed with gradual relaxation. Layla touched the tiny curled hand, which squeezed instinctively and relaxed again into sleep. She put her finger into the corner of the quivering pink mouth to loosen the tight hold on her breast, then sat up carefully into the chill, moving Baby to her shoulder to make sure all bubbles were released before she set the child down for a few more hours.

Love would come. The deep bond would just have to be forged if it wasn't going to show up on its own. She couldn't worry, couldn't waste energy torturing herself. Everything was worse in the dark before dawn. Time would take care of it.

She rubbed Baby's back and felt the vibration in the tiny body a second before it traveled up and burst out in a belch that would make a football team applaud. Layla smiled and felt a welling of tenderness. "Atta girl."

She slid down under the warm covers again and faced Baby away from her, bringing her knees up to surround the child with her body. She didn't really need to get up yet. It wouldn't be light for a couple of hours still. Wood to chop today and bread to bake. Her supplies would hold out for a few more days before she had to make the monthly trek to Leavenworth for more. As much as she hated leaving the security of her cabin, clean laundry wouldn't hurt. And she could stand one of the strawberry milkshakes Mrs. Brody made at the Corner Creamery. Nice, also, to check in with Alice Cranston who managed Gone to Pottery, the store in Leavenworth that sold Layla's pieces, and who handled the public-contact aspects of her custom pottery business.

But overall, having no one around, having her cabin and her clay and her potter's wheel and kiln, the woods and birds and rabbits and raccoon and deer, the mountains, and now most especially Baby, was the best thing going. The rest of the world could disappear in a puff of smoke and it wouldn't matter to her at all. After all those years of moving and adjusting and suffering and coping, her life and how she spent it was entirely up to her.

She yawned and snuggled closer to the tiny form next to her, making sure the sheet was smooth and firm under Baby's nose. And no one could take any of that away.

CHAPTER TWO

BRETT DEVLIN TURNED WEST onto US-2, tapping the steering wheel in time to an Ella Fitzgerald CD, and crossed the Columbia River on his way to Leavenworth, Washington. A light snow was falling, coating the pines to a frosted green, blowing in skittish patterns across the highway. Dry snow, not hazardous conditions, but enough to make sure he couldn't relax on this final leg of his two-day journey.

He could have flown into Seattle and rented a car. He would have saved some time. But Seattle meant Shana and their newfound stepsister, Alexandra. She'd appeared out of the blue, the daughter of Jonathan Webber, aka Gary Devlin, the man who'd adopted Brett and Shana after their Mom had kicked their own father out of the house. Shana had jumped at the chance for a family reunion, as she seemed to think it was. Dropped her whole life to move up there and work in Alexandra's child-care center.

He couldn't for the life of him understand that logic or why Alexandra would travel all the way to Nebraska to invite him—someone she didn't know from Adam—to her *wedding*, for God's sake, as if he were one of her dearest friends.

Brett tightened his grip on the steering wheel as a gust of wind caught his pickup and threatened to take over the job of steering. Shana was his sister and he loved her. They'd been through childhood together, had faced upheaval and survived, bonded. This Alexandra woman was connected to them purely by accident, and Shana expected him to embrace her as a long-lost sibling?

Sorry. It took more than legal ties to make someone family. Which was damn ironic, given the errand he was on right now. He'd tracked Layla Marino as far as Leavenworth, three hours east of Seattle, a damn odd place for someone who'd had her baby up in Glacier, near the Canadian border, to live. Not surprisingly, the police hadn't been able to find her. No address in Leavenworth, no record of a driver's license or car registration, but apparently she supplied wares to a shop, Gone to Pottery, run by a woman in town, so she couldn't live too far from there.

He'd called the woman, Alice Cranston, pretending to be interested in purchasing one of Ms. Marino's astonishingly expensive custom-made creations, and had met with the expected stone wall when his questions about the artist got personal. All he'd managed to get out of her, in his patented roundabout method of questioning, was that Layla lived in a cabin secluded in the mountains. Didn't seem to care much for the society of her fellow humans.

Terrific. Shana would be thrilled to give Chris up to some flaky hermit in the middle of nowhere.

He'd made a reservation for tonight at the Linderhof Motor Inn, expecting to stay a day, maybe two. Finding Ms. Marino shouldn't be hard. Telling her that the child she'd taken into her home and heart wasn't hers would be harder. Telling her she'd have to give the child up would be hardest.

Delivering bad news was one of the least attractive

parts of his job. He squinted through the snow at the spectacular mountain scenery ahead of him. Driving through this fabulous part of the country instead of being chained to a desk, pushing paper for some corporate machine more than made up for it. Using his brain to get inside people's heads, to take apparently unrelated evidence and form it into a beautiful complete picture was even better.

He turned off the CD as he came to the town, which lay nestled in the Icicle Valley by the Wenatchee River. He wanted to approach in silence, let his senses soak up the atmosphere without distraction. Stunning. Not that he'd leave Nebraska, his home since birth, but this was some serious scenery. The valley greenery had been dusted by snow that glowed gray-blue in the deepening twilight; the lights of the tiny town sparkled against the backdrop of the mountains, rising dark and silent so far above and beyond. The kind of sight that made you glad to be alive—and sorry that so many idiots were.

He followed directions he'd printed off the Internet, parked at the inn and headed to the office, enjoying the sharp, cold air and sweet, natural scents, the gradually easing movement of his stiff body after ten hours locked in a stale truck. Tomorrow, first thing, he'd get in touch with this Alice person. Then he'd find Ms. Artsy Marino and put in motion a chain of events that would change her life forever.

LAYLA DROVE PAST her driveway and went up to the circular turnaround marking the end of the mountaintop road. Unfortunately, her tracks would be easy to follow now that the snow had stopped, though Leavenworth locals had warned her of another approaching storm. She turned around and backtracked, trying to keep her tires in the ruts she'd already made. At the mouth of her driveway, she put the vehicle in park and got out, careful not to slam the door and wake Baby.

A log lay haphazardly across the entrance to the rough road—her camouflage. She dragged it aside, grunting with the effort, and climbed back into her jeep. A few yards in toward her house, she stopped again, replaced the log and did her best to cover up the tracks on the road that showed she'd turned. Too bad she didn't have a remote control gizmo like Batman in the TV series, so she could press a button and have the woods open and close behind her moving car, leaving no trace.

Maybe she was being paranoid, but after what happened last year, paranoid felt a lot better than vulnerable. She clapped her sheepskin mittens together to clear off the snow and bits of bark and headed back to the car. Close to the house, she parked and unloaded her supplies: meat, rice, flour, pasta, beans, cereal, dried fruit and apples, bags of potatoes and root vegetables, kerosene, a few sweet and perishable treats… Her usual monthly haul.

She drove the old, squeaky jeep her grandparents left her along with the cabin into the parking area across the clearing behind the cabin so the vehicle would be pretty well hidden from the house. During the day, when she looked out her windows, she wanted to see woods and ferns, birds and squirrels, not metal and glass and rubber.

Arrived at last, she got out of the car and paused to listen before she unbuckled Baby from her car seat. Coming back from town always made her jittery. She couldn't quite shake the fear that she was being followed again. That someone else might have spotted her and figured a woman alone in the woods needed a male forced on her. Pigs, most of them. Growing up, she'd seen plenty of what men were capable of, what drove them. Tall and blond in a migrant community meant she attracted some unwelcome attention from the locals, though the workers themselves had treated her for the most part with respect.

The good news was that she had learned at a young age to stay tough, watchful, and to fight dirty. The smirking creep who followed her last year had turned on his expensive city boots and gone yelping down the mountain with more than just his male pride wounded. She'd been careful since then, compulsively checking her mirror for pursuers every time she started the trek home from Leavenworth. For months after that incident she'd been terrified he'd come back to finish his business, this time more angry than horny. Nothing had come of it. He was probably a tourist and wouldn't bother her again. But she couldn't shake the unease, or the anger that he'd violated her sense of security and isolation, what she cherished most about living here.

As different from the constant moving and change and crowds of her youth as she could get.

She lifted Baby cautiously onto her shoulder, praying the little one would stay asleep until Layla got her purchases put away and had a cup of tea. The visits to town exhausted her. The quaint town of Leavenworth was hardly a bustling metropolis, but negotiating the streets and shops with an infant, making sure she forgot nothing so she wouldn't have to return before next month, delivering her pottery and picking up orders for the next batch… Draining. While being

here, alone on her mountaintop in a well-stocked
house with a blizzard on the way, energized her. No
one around to judge or to criticize, no one around to
make her feel as though she didn't belong. Paradise.
She thanked her late grandfather every day for saving
this slice of heaven for her twenty-first birthday in-
heritance.

Baby made an impossibly adorable cooing sound;
her head lolled up, then relaxed back onto Layla's
shoulder, nestled in that spot between neck and shoulder that seemed made for an infant's head. Layla eased
herself into the cabin and bent to lay her daughter in
her crib, keeping the contact between their bodies until
the last possible second to minimize chances of Baby
missing the warmth and waking up.

To her profound relief, Baby settled, one arm up
over her head and one out to the side, like an infant
fencer. Layla smiled, tenderness welling up in her
heart. Her daughter. No more middle-of-the-night anx-
ieties. Mother and daughter were doing fine.

She turned from the crib to the sacks of groceries
sitting on the rag rug in the middle of her kitchen area
and pushed up her sleeves.

Twenty minutes later, everything was put away—
baking goods on the baking shelf, pasta sorted by
shape, tall items in back, shorter in front. She carefully
wiped out the refrigerator, which she defrosted during
her trips to town, started it again with a blow torch,
and took her time packing the tiny freezer so as much
fit as possible, trying one package here, another there,
like a jigsaw puzzle.

Finally satisfied, she folded the paper bags and nestled them in the wooden magazine holder near the fireplace, then swept the area carefully and surveyed her

neat, orderly, cabin with pride and relief to have the trip over with. Good for another month.

She crossed back to the kitchen, filled the kettle from the cold water tap and turned on the stove. The flame caught, then sputtered. There was plenty of gas. She'd gotten two bottles last month. Must be time to switch the tanks.

She went outside, crossing her arms over her chest against the cold air that treated her sweater like an insignificant obstacle to its quest to chill her skin. Behind the house on flat blocks of wood, the two tanks stood like inert pewter-colored torpedoes. She reached up on tiptoe, twisted the knob shut on the empty tank and opened the knob on the full one. Next trip into town she'd need a new supply. She probably should have—

Layla froze, then ducked and crouched behind the tanks. A noise. Footsteps. How to get to Baby? How to get to her gun?

Someone was out there.

BRETT STOPPED HIS TRUCK at the end of the main road—a track, really, that had wound him up and around this damn mountain for the better part of the afternoon—and frowned at the circling tire marks in the snow. She'd turned around, but she hadn't made it all the way back down the mountain. He'd been following only one set of tracks on the way up. He cursed himself for his carelessness. Wherever she'd doubled back would now be ruined by the treads of his own tires. Where had she gone off the road?

He circled the Chevy around and drove slowly back down the way he'd come, peering right and left for signs of disturbed snow or a road back in the woods.

Twenty yards later, he found what he'd been looking for. A good job of camouflage. She'd tried to erase her tracks, but anyone looking for the driveway could find it easily. Anyone not looking would doubtless assume the main road led to nowhere. Very clever.

He'd managed to get a general idea of this Marino woman from her business associate, Alice, and from casual conversation with the gossipy woman who ran the Corner Creamery. Layla had lived here nearly eight years, rarely came to town, had shown up pregnant last year, with no sign of the father before or after.

According to Alice, she'd disappeared for the birth, had gone north to have the baby, though no one quite knew why. People figured she lived fine with her pottery business and the money her grandfather had left her. They'd all expected her to last about three weeks when she first moved up there, barely old enough to drink. She always came to the Corner Creamery on her trips into town and had a large strawberry milkshake. She was quiet, polite and acted most of the time as if she wished she were invisible.

Brett could picture that perfectly. Probably some minor mental disturbance, maybe a form of autism, which made living among her fellow humans unpleasant. An artist, balancing the strength of her creative power with weak or deficient social skills.

He put the Chevy in park, debating which would scare her more—approach by car or on foot. A breeze whipped snow around the fallen log across her driveway, probably obscuring her tracks further. Good thing he'd followed her fairly closely. Amazing luck that his presence coincided with one of her monthly trips to town. Considering the maze of roads on these mountains, he'd have had a hell of a time finding her on his own. In fact he might never make it back, except that "down" was always a good bet.

He switched off the engine and climbed from the truck, shutting the door gently behind him. He'd go in on foot. Less threatening to her on her own territory than showing up in a huge vehicle. He didn't want to scare her to ground like a terrified rabbit. She'd probably catch one glimpse of him and bolt into the house. God knows he had to approach her gently, gain the poor thing's trust to tell her this unsettling news. No telling how she'd react, especially if she turned out to be unbalanced. Probably crumple into a helpless heap and he'd have to sit and pat her hand for an hour before he could—

"Get the hell off my land or I'll blow away your brains and ego with one shot."

His body stiffened, instincts and senses in immediate overdrive. Holy hell. Apparently he was not going to be dealing with a terrified rabbit. He didn't particularly care for unbalanced people with guns. Unless she was bluffing.

He turned slowly so as not to annoy or startle her, and discovered with sickening certainty that she wasn't bluffing. The serious end of a shotgun was firmly pointed at what the woman obviously considered the source of male brains and ego, but what he called something else entirely. The cool rage in her eyes made it a pretty sure bet she was prepared to back up her words with her trigger finger.

Brett put his hands up tentatively, making sure he appeared confused and submissive. "Is that a typical Washington welcome?"

"You're from out of state." The words came out

clipped and murderous. Apparently being from out of state was bad.

"Nebraska." He studied her carefully. Slightly taller than average, younger than he was—twenty-nine if the woman at the Creamery's guess was correct. Her blond hair was clean, clothes worn but not ratty. He couldn't tell the color of her eyes—light brown or hazel—but they were clear and steady, so if she was off her rocker, she was only just off the edge, not sprawled on the floor next to it.

"What the hell are you doing here?"

He gave a slight smile, pleasant instead of mocking, though he'd rather indulge the latter. "Could we have this discussion when my…brains and ego aren't being targeted? I know it sounds strange, but having a weapon pointed at my crotch doesn't put me at ease."

She didn't smile. Her expression didn't soften at all. The gun didn't waver. Her breath came out into the November chill in frequent white puffs. "I'm not interested in your comfort. What are you doing on my land?"

"I want to talk to you."

"Oh?" The word was soft but the accompanying sneer said loud and clear that she didn't believe him for a second.

"Just talk."

"I'm listening."

He clenched his teeth. This wasn't exactly the venue he'd had in mind. "I'd rather talk where it's warm and I'm not in danger of being mutilated."

"*No.*" Her voice rose into near hysteria and she took two deep breaths to get herself back under control. "You are not coming in my house."

Brett narrowed his eyes. Unless he was wrong,

which he could be, though he generally read people well, right now Layla Marino wasn't just some nutcase xenophobe defending her property. He'd seen this kind of hostile fear plenty of times. Something had happened with some other stranger that was feeding her fear and anger. His best hope of getting her to listen was to tackle that head-on.

He held his hands higher, took a step closer, keeping a sharp eye on the gun and monitoring the tension increasing in her body. "I'm not here to hurt you."

"Then what the hell are you here for?"

"I told you. I want to talk to you."

"Bull."

"You've heard that before? Someone said they just wanted to talk, and they didn't?"

"What do you mean by that?"

He calculated and chose the safe path. "I hope he got what he deserved instead of what he wanted."

"None of your damn business." The gun wavered and lowered slightly. For the first time she looked directly into his eyes instead of at him, and incredibly, standing in the snowy woods with his feet feeling like Good Humor treats and a weapon pointed toward one of his favorite body parts, Brett felt a flicker of attraction. Not just attraction, but that mysterious flicker of connection, of pull between two people that scientists had never quite been able to explain, and probably never would.

Layla cleared her throat and shot him a vicious look as if she'd forgotten her fury for a moment and had to make sure he knew it was still there. "He got what he deserved."

Brett's body relaxed back to its previous level of tension. He couldn't explain his relief. Some of it was professional—if she'd been raped, her distrust and fear would be all that much harder to get past. But some of it was purely…male. And he wasn't going to examine that any more than it needed to be, which was not at all. "Good for you."

"You'll get the same if you don't get out of here."

He let the silence linger, let her harsh words disappear into the snowy woods so they'd be totally disconnected from his response. "I came here to talk to you, Layla."

Immediately she clenched the gun back into its deadly aim. "How do you know my name?"

"Layla Marino. Last known address in—"

She stiffened and glanced back toward the house. He focused on the structure and then he heard it. A child wailing.

Layla turned back to him, clearly agitated. "You have to leave—"

"The baby needs you."

"I can hear that." She spoke through gritted teeth. "Get out of here now."

He folded his arms across his chest and adopted a spread-legged stance, an indication of stubborn settling-in. Snow began falling again, tiny soft flakes that drifted through the trees. "Go to the child. I'll wait."

She twisted her mouth in indecision, glanced once more back at her cabin and gave a quick nod. "Okay."

He lifted an eyebrow in surprise. Okay? Ms. Annie Oakley had given in? Just like that?

She took one step back, then in a quick, seemingly careless motion, raised the shotgun and fired at his fly.

The bullet passed harmlessly between his legs, but

the shot made him yell and jerk backward, trip over a fallen log and land on his butt in the snow.

"Are you crazy? You could have killed me."

The minute the shout left his lips, an absurd cliché of outrage, she laughed, a cold humorless sound.

"If I'd wanted to hit you, I would have. I'm going inside to my baby. If you're not gone by the time I get back, I'll shoot again. And this time I won't miss."

She turned her back to him and strode across the clearing toward her house without glancing again in his direction.

Brett dragged himself to his feet, heart still hammering, breath only starting to come back under control. Crazy woman. He swung around and stared behind him in disbelief. A small pine had nearly been severed. He could barely stand looking at the gaping wound. Damn crazy woman.

The door to her cabin slammed shut behind her. An indignant I'm-done-with-you thud. The sound set him off. To hell with her. He slapped the snow off his soggy rear and stalked to his pickup, back turned to the cabin and Layla Marino. *To hell with her.* He wasn't going to risk getting his balls shot off so she could have the news about her baby broken to her gently. Jackhammering it into her skull was too gentle. He'd driven for two solid days and spent two more trying to find her for his sister's sake. All to spare a cold-hearted crazy woman some small measure of heartache. The news was the same whether he gave it to her or the proper authorities did.

He should have listened to his instincts in the beginning and told Shana he wanted no part of it. He'd call Jaron, tell him where Ms. Marino lived, and let the Seattle P.D. do their own freaking dirty work.

Layla Marino could just deal with it. He was having nothing more to do with her.

CHAPTER THREE

LAYLA CLOSED HER EYES and leaned back in the maple rocker she'd exchanged with a local artisan for some of her own work, trying desperately to relax enough to allow Baby to feed. Without relaxation, her milk wouldn't flow, no matter how badly she or Baby wanted it to. She could sense the child's anxiety, in reaction to her own, compounded by the unfamiliar lack of food in response to the usual stimulation.

Breathe, Layla. Baby needs you. Breathe. Forget about him. Forget about what happened.

She went inside herself, instructed her body to relax progressively, the way the pregnancy book had taught her in preparation for labor. Breathe...and relax, breathe...and relax. Toes...ankles...calves...

Baby pulled back from her breast, gave a cry of frustration and latched on again. Layla rocked, breathed, relaxed. Chest...shoulders...neck.

The burning tingle in her breast and Baby's ravenous gulping sent her the happy signal. *Eureka, we have lactation.*

She settled back, prepared to enjoy the hormones produced by breastfeeding, which usually sent her body into a delicious peaceful state. Unfortunately her mind seemed to have developed an efficient, whirling immunity.

What had he wanted? Why had he followed her?

Had she managed to scare him off? Was he still out there? Would he wait as he'd threatened to?

She opened her eyes and peeked at her gun—dubbed Jake, for no particular reason except that the name sounded tough and dependable—which she'd leaned against the wall within easy reach. If he tried to break down the door, she'd have the weapon out and pointed at him within seconds. This time if he tried anything, she'd let him have it for real.

Somehow, though, and she was operating only on instinct here, she didn't think he would. He hadn't leered or given off hostile vibes—well, not until she'd shot at him, but she couldn't exactly blame him for that. He'd been cautious, respectful, and he'd kept his calm. As if having a shotgun pointed at him wasn't his favorite activity, but also not one that was completely strange to him.

A cop under cover? He'd had on a black leather jacket, black jeans, black boots. An attractive guy. Tall and lean. Too sophisticated for a Nebraska farm boy. He gave the impression of power and authority without having to act tough. She'd bet he was used to action, not desk work.

What would a cop want from her? She had no family left, so there'd be no need to contact her over the death of a relative. She'd never been to Nebraska, had no connections there that she knew of. Maybe someone she used to know had moved there and gotten into trouble? Maybe he wanted her as a character witness? Who knew?

She could picture him out there, waiting no matter how long it took. In the picture in her mind he looked stubborn, but not threatening. Stubborn and cold. Stubborn and cold with a butt wet from tripping over a log.

She smiled down at Baby, who was blissfully full now, but still sucking for the comfort and closeness. "What do you think?"

Baby shifted her gaze up toward Layla's voice, then blinked slowly and kept nursing.

"Think we can trust him at least far enough to hear what he has to say?"

Baby lifted her head off the breast and graced her mom with a smile that involved her entire face and most of her body.

Layla nodded and grinned back. "Okay, we'll finish up here, then we'll go back out there with Jake for protection and give this guy a chance. One false move on his part, though, and you can learn a valuable lesson from Mom about how to handle men."

She put Baby to her shoulder and patted her warm, impossibly small back until the appropriate volcanic gas action took place, followed by the rushing gurgle of a filling diaper.

"Lovely." Layla grinned at the satisfied look on Baby's face. "You are a regular finishing-school charmer."

Baby beamed back and allowed herself to be put on the changing pad without fuss. Layla started the all-too-familiar procedure with fumbling fingers and forced herself to slow down. Why rush? She was in no hurry. Let him stay out there until he was good and icy.

She imagined him growing impatient in the now steadily falling snow, maybe pacing back and forth, muttering unkind things about her under his breath. She smiled a slow, mischievous and thoroughly enjoyable smile. The look on his face when he'd heard the gun go off was priceless. All his macho cool, all his I'm-in-charge confidence, had ducked and run squealing for cover. At the very least when she went back out there, he'd know she was a person to be reckoned with.

Baby let out a squeak and series of adorable nonsense noises. Layla redressed her, and keeping one protecting hand on the soft wiggly body, reached over to the little red, green and blue snowsuit lying across the chair she'd salvaged and caned herself last summer. She'd splurged on the suit on a previous trip to Leavenworth. As a newborn, Baby was fine wrapped in a quilt and secured in the light-framed baby backpack Layla carried her around in, but now that the child had found seriously strong kicking legs, she needed more reliable coverage.

Layla pushed the appropriate reluctant baby body parts into their proper places in the suit, whooshed up the zipper, smiling at Baby's delight—and had to tell herself again to slow down. Layla had something the guy wanted. He'd made the trip from Nebraska to see her. He wasn't going anywhere.

She put her own coat on—not nearly as cute as Baby's, and worn and a bit grimy from outdoor living, now that she noticed—took down the backpack from its nail by the door, opened the frame and set it on the floor. Baby slid in after a few disagreements as to where her legs belonged, and Layla hoisted the whole contraption onto her shoulders. She went back to grab Jake and glanced out the window into the thickening snow, knowing the man was too close to the road to be visible from the house, but not able to help herself.

She put her hand to the doorknob, unable to slow her too-fast heart, squeezed Jake's comforting cold metal, took one quick deep breath and yanked open the door. Ready or not, here she came.

Baby gave a squeal as they stepped out into the woods, and followed it with a garbled string of almost-syllables. Layla gave a distracted, approving mom response and walked down the drive, body moving with a muscle-binding combination of eagerness and hesitancy, eyes fixed on the spot where she'd left him. Around one more stand of trees and she would glimpse him again, all in black like some urban commando. He even had dark hair, down to his collar, and dark penetrating eyes to complete the picture. A face that probably made women swoon. Most women. Layla didn't do the swoon thing.

She rounded the trees, jaw tight, breath held in anticipation, Jake brought up horizontal. Then stopped. Where was the damn guy? She swung to the right, toward the road, and then around three-sixty, the hair on her nape prickling, nerves receptive, hearing acute. A few more steps toward the road. Where the hell was he?

The wind picked up and blew a white swirl into their faces. Baby let out a brief wail, then quieted. Layla blew out a breath. *Atta girl. A tough lady, like her mom. Loved being outside, even in the beginnings of a storm.*

She reached the road and stood, Jake dangling at her side, looking up one way then down the other, back and forth like a complete fool, as if he might appear if she only looked enough times. She forced her attention to the road. The snow was already freshening and softening the tire tracks, but she could see clearly that he'd driven back down the mountain. There wasn't even a snow-free rectangle where his car had been parked, which meant he'd left shortly after she'd shot at him, before the snow had started in earnest.

Layla let out a short, bitter laugh. Guess he hadn't been quite as tough and/or persistent as he made himself out to be. She stayed there on the road, struggling with some emotion that felt a little too much like disappointment.

Okay, maybe she'd been half looking forward to a showdown. Maybe she'd been curious as to what had brought him all this way. But wasn't it much better that he had cleared out, tail between his legs?

A gust of wind turned the soft tickle of snow into a gritty attack; Baby gave another wail, longer this time, before she returned to pioneer infant stoicism. Layla turned to walk back to the cabin. Who was she kidding? She'd won the first round, but her instinct about the man told her that scaring him away would take more than a warning shot. She could be wrong, but her intuition rarely failed, even if she didn't get to use it on people much anymore. She'd sleep with Jake close to her bed tonight.

If he knew her name, then whatever he had to say was meant for her ears and he would try again.

Her stomach tensed at the thought. A sitting duck. Here in her mountaintop sanctuary, her peaceful escape from the world, she was victim to the whims of someone who wanted her and knew exactly where she was. Damn him for not living up to his stubborn promise so she could be done with his business and go back to being anonymous and unreachable. The way she liked her life.

Layla walked past the last place she'd seen Captain Commando, remembering him before she shot at him, standing purposeful and unyielding all in black. A man like that wouldn't take humiliation lightly. He'd probably left to toy with her. To take power back into his own hands by making her wait and wonder. He'd be back, damn him, on his own time, on his own schedule.

And there wasn't a thing on God's snowy mountain that she could do about it.

BRETT TOOK ANOTHER TURN on the crazy maze of unmarked mountain roads. People around here must have maps tattooed on their butts at birth. How the hell anyone could maneuver on a level other than roads-that-go-up and roads-that-go-down, he hadn't a clue.

His pickup did a quick slide on a snowy patch. He was driving too fast for the weather, but between his lingering anger at Shotgun Marino and the urge to get through this quickly intensifying storm to the safety of the hotel, he didn't much care. He was used to snow in Nebraska. But not on narrow curving roads.

He turned on the radio, found a local station and hoped for a weather update. Another uncomfortable curve around a forested crag, another fork in the road, another decision. Down. The down fork. A no-brainer. He hoped. This had all been much easier when he was following the tracks left by Layla's Jeep. He should have been throwing a trail of pebbles out the window the whole time, like Hansel and Gretel, to show him the way home. He had taken pains to note landmarks on the way up, but with the snow cutting visibility and the wind picking up, he'd just have to wing it.

His satellite phone rang. He took a quick look down to locate it on the seat next to him at the same time his pickup hit another icy patch. The Chevy did a slow, graceful pirouette across the road and came to rest with its right rear wheel tilted down into a ditch.

Damn.

The phone rang again. He sighed and punched it on. "Devlin."

"It's your sister. What's going on?"

He nursed the accelerator to move the car forward and made a sound of exasperation when the wheels spun uselessly on the snow-slick surface. "Oh, nothing. I'm in the middle of Northwest Nowhere, Washington, in a blinding snowstorm and my truck just ran off the road."

"Oh, Brett!"

His anger quickly changed into the need to reassure her. "It's okay. The truck's fine. I'll get it going."

"Are you sure? Do you want me to call—"

"No." He rolled his eyes. His sister was a walking rescue operation. "I'll be fine. If I can't get it moving, I'll call someone myself."

"Okay…"

He pictured her silent impatience and took pity. "Yes, I found her."

"Oh, Brett! I knew you could!"

He snorted at her little-sister faith in him, though he couldn't help feeling pleased. "She's a piece of work."

"In what way?"

"She shot at me." He struggled out of the cab, turned his collar up against the stinging crystals of snow and surveyed the situation.

"*What?*"

He winced and pushed the phone from his ear at her indignant shriek. "Chip on her shoulder a mile wide. Seems she has a history with unwanted male visitors trying to ruin her life. Only the guy before me had designs on her body instead of her child.''

''Oh, God, the poor thing. No wonder she shot you. I can't say I blame her.''

His brows shot up. *''Excuse me?''*

''Wouldn't you be wary if you were her?''

''Sure I'd be wary.'' He reached his foot under the Chevy and cleared away snow in front of his tires, stabbing and stepping with his boot. ''But there's a huge leap between wary and bullets.''

''I'm sure she wasn't really trying to hit you.''

''As a matter of fact, no.'' He walked back to the driver's side and gave his tires a satisfying kick to get the snow off his boots before he climbed back into the cab. Shana always looked for the good in people, and to her credit, she often found it. ''Ms. Marino wasn't trying to hit me. Just wanted me to know any plans I might have for future sexual activity were hers to ruin.''

''I don't understand what you—'' Shana skipped a beat, then gave a sudden snort of amusement. ''She aimed *there?*''

He narrowed his eyes. ''What is so—''

''Ha!'' His sister burst into a gale of laughter. ''I love this woman.''

Brett glared hard at the stand of pines to his right, ghostly in the swirling white. *Ha, ha. Very funny.*

''Listen, I don't—''

''God, I can just picture it. You showing up all intent on being kind and breaking this news to her gently, probably expecting her to be some meek little thing, and instead she's this mountain woman who scares the hell out of you with a gun aimed at your...privates.''

She went off into another spasm of hilarity.

"Enough." His mouth twitched in spite of himself.

"I'm sorry. I'm sorry." She gasped with the effort of bringing her laughter under control. "Okay. Whew."

"I'm glad this is so fun for you." He was smiling now, he couldn't help himself. His sister had a real talent for keeping him from taking himself too seriously.

"So when are you going back?"

His smile died. "When am I *what?*"

"Going back. As in returning. As in buying a bulletproof jock strap and trying again."

"Shana." He used his best, patient big-brother voice. "I happen to like my 'privates,' as you call them. I have grown fond of them over the years. They work. They give women pleasure. They give *me* pleasure. Strangely, I am somewhat hesitant to volunteer them for target practice."

"You're...not going back?" Her voice turned hesitant and wobbly.

He sighed, leaned his elbow on the window and lowered his head into his hand. "Shana, think about it. The woman is hostile to strangers. I don't have days to gain her trust. I'd have to tell her just as quickly and impersonally as a police officer would. After our last encounter, she'd probably take it a lot better from the proper authorities."

"Brett, please." Her voice sounded strangely bouncy and he realized she was walking through Keith's town house. "You drove all the way out there. You found her. Unless you think she's unbalanced..."

He pictured Layla's clear eyes, her steady hand. The strong mixture of fear and pride and desperate courage. No, she wasn't crazy. Weird, maybe—who wouldn't be, living up in the middle of nowhere. But not crazy.

"I don't think she's unbalanced." He spoke wearily, knowing what was coming next.

"You sound sorry she's not."

"I am."

"Why?"

He ran his hand over his face, trying to dispel the image of Layla, tough and vulnerable, alone in the woods with her baby and her gun.

"Because I know you're going to convince me to go back there."

"Damn straight." A soft, painfully innocent cooing noise came over the phone and Brett rolled his eyes. The woman was a champ. She was making sure he could hear the baby. Making sure he understood there was a little life involved. "I know the cops can tell her, Brett. But I want you to do it. I know you'll find a way that will make it easy on this woman."

"Shana, cops are trained for this, not only breaking the news, but dealing with the aftermath. What makes you think—"

"I don't think. I know. Please do this for me." Another little coo, followed by an experimental baby screech. "Please do it for Chris."

He grabbed a handful of his hair. "You are a pro, Shana."

"I know." She started humming to the child and he pictured her rocking the little girl. The little girl who was Layla's birth daughter.

"You really want Chris to grow up in a cabin at the top of a mountain with a wild-woman mother?"

"I really want to put right what went wrong. That's what this is about."

Brett tightened his mouth and stared up at the ceiling of his truck. He wasn't so sure he agreed that this was the right thing to do. But if the child's uncle wanted the baby Layla had, his own flesh and blood, then he had a right to fight for her.

"Okay."

"Oh, Brett." Shana's voice came out on a trembling sigh. "Thanks."

"Yeah, whatever." He said goodbye and punched off the phone. A sappy country song ended and the announcer's voice came on. Winter storm advisory for the next two days. One to two feet of snow. Blizzard conditions on the way. Icy temperatures expected for the next week.

A gust of wind rocked his truck. Brett squinted out into the drifting whiteness, soon to fade into the gray of evening. Two days of this and the worst was yet to come. He'd go nuts cooling his heels in the hotel. And who knew how long before the plows made it up as far as her cabin, or even if they did. Better to go back now, tell her, and drive down before the snow got too deep, before the storm got too bad.

Relieved to have a definite plan, Brett got out of the truck and stepped into the woods to collect pine branches to wedge in front of his tires for traction. The wind bit into his cheeks, drove snow down between his collar and his neck.

He managed to get the pickup moving back up the mountain, and followed the barely visible tracks he'd left on his way down.

Half an hour later he recognized the final turn onto the road that led by Layla Marino's camouflaged driveway. He pulled the steering wheel to the left. Nothing happened. The truck kept drifting straight, toward a clump of firs. He straightened the wheel, tapped the brake, turned the wheel again, this time accelerating gently. To his relief, the truck turned— and in sickening slow motion, slid sideways off the road and came to rest tipped against the smooth bark of the trees.

Damn again.

He unbuckled his seat belt, threw open the door and climbed out of the tilted cab, feeling as though he was scrabbling up the deck of the *Titanic*.

More damn pine boughs. More wet snow on his pants. More snow down his collar. More hatred for mountains and the Pacific Northwest.

After another long hour of stuck-truck excitement, his hands scraped raw and icy-cold, the light starting to fade into evening around him, he admitted defeat. This job required a tow truck. He wasn't even going to think about how long it would be before he could get one up here. Right now he just wanted to be warm. Even if it was in the house of a woman who wanted to remove his masculinity.

He started walking up the road, arms crossed to keep his hands protected, cursing the wet and cold that seemed to have seeped in everywhere. Twenty or thirty yards up the road, he cut into the woods to get some relief from the wind and driving snow. He squinted ahead and to the left to get his bearings, and struck out toward the direction he thought right, stumbling occasionally on rocks and branches hidden by the soft covering of white.

He sure as hell hoped she had coffee. A big steaming mug to wrap his sore hands around. Preferably laced with brandy. A thick wool blanket and a tub of hot water for his frozen feet. Armchair. Crackling fire. Something for his empty stomach. He skirted a bunch of trees. Was that a structure up ahead? Looked too small to be her cabin, but he must be getting close. He leaped lightly over a log. If he could just get past her urge to shoot him, he—

Pain seared through his ankle as he landed on uneven ground. His knees buckled and he twisted his body to land on his shoulder. His foot caught on a branch and he went over backward instead, arms out, helpless to stop his fall. His head struck a rocky outcrop and he lay there dazed, staring at the white pinpoint flakes falling toward his face.

Double damn.

A few seconds later, blinking to try to clear his murky head, movements unsteady, he managed to roll to sitting. His injured ankle, under a good-size branch, refused to roll with him. He let out a yell and sat panting, cursing the pain. His vision sparked with black and white spots. He slumped down, helpless to stop the blood draining from his head, and watched the frozen white woods around him blur and slowly turn to black.

CHAPTER FOUR

LAYLA GLANCED OUT the darkening window at the driving lines of gray-white that shifted and swirled with the whim of the wind. She rocked Baby, smiling at her lovely eyes, which were at the moment tiny slits, getting tinier with each slow-motion blink. On stormy evenings like these, Layla loved her cabin best. Gas lamps lit the simple pine walls with a soft yellow glow, and the fire behind the woodstove's glass door sent shapes and shadows dancing through the room. The fury outside wrapped the warm interior around her like a protective blanket.

Baby's eyelids made the descent into sleep, sprang open once more, then closed with finality. Layla rocked her for another few minutes, partly to be sure she was completely settled, and partly because it did a body so much good to hold a warm sleeping child. Must be genetic programming that made it so fabulous. Nature's way of making sure children were protected at their most vulnerable.

Eventually, however, the growl of her stomach and the call of her bladder got her up to place Baby in her crib. The child would waken for one more feeding before Layla herself went to bed.

She put water on the stove to boil for her usual pasta dinner, and checked Baby one more time before zipping up her parka and heading into the havoc outside to visit the outhouse. She'd have to make sure to toilet train Baby in the summertime.

One step out her door, the wind whipped away her breath and drove angry crystals to sting her face. She bent her head and trudged through the fresh powder to the outhouse, about fifty feet from her cabin. Near the structure, she paused, lifted her head and glanced around her. Something wasn't right. Immediately she thought of Captain Commando, then just as immediately squelched all but a nagging bit of the thought. He'd certainly struck her as stubborn and determined, but he'd have to be all that plus a total idiot to pick a night like this for a drive back up the mountain.

She went into the outhouse, did her business and stepped back out, pulling on a mitten that slid grudgingly over her hand, still damp from the hand sanitizer. The door latch clunked faintly into place behind her and she took two steps toward the house before stopping again. Something wasn't right. Something...

She pulled her hood down so her ears could hear the woods instead of the rhythmic swish of nylon that followed her steps.

Still nothing, but her instincts were on red alert, ears straining, senses operating at full capacity.

Two steps back toward the house, a careful scan of the woods around her... Squinting through the swirling white, she saw him. Her fight-or-flight mechanism kicked in big-time, followed immediately by wary concern. A man. The total idiot after all. Lying on his stomach with a powdery coating of fresh snow over his back. Was he dead? Passed out? Injured? Why the hell had he left and come back now?

She walked cautiously closer, peering through the dense snow, and frowned at the jagged compacted trail behind him. How far had he dragged himself? She couldn't see more than a foot or two behind him. About a yard from his head, she stopped and squatted cautiously. Not dead. Breathing hard, in fact. His head lifted suddenly and she gave a yell and fell backward onto her butt.

"'s that you?" His face contracted in pain. Layla could barely hear his voice over a roaring gust of wind. "Need help."

She reacted instinctively, crawling forward at the same time suspicion wanted to hold her back. "Where are you hurt?"

"Head." He panted from the effort of speaking. "Ankle. Truck's stuck. I fell."

A gust of wind blew snow off the ground. He lowered his face back down to avoid the assault.

Layla shifted beside him and leaned forward to touch his hair. If he was faking, she was going to string him up by his privates. Then shoot him down.

The egg-size lump on the back of his head changed her suspicion into grudging action. The man had invaded her privacy, threatened her peace of mind, and now she'd be stuck taking *care* of him, for God's sake.

"Put your arm around me. I'll get you inside. How long have you been out here?"

He groaned. "Three or four weeks. Minimum."

Her mouth twitched in spite of herself and she helped drape his arm around her neck. Tough guy using humor when he probably wanted to curl up and sleep. He was damn lucky she found him, though he was strong enough that he might have made it to her cabin on his own. "Can you stand?"

He nodded and got to his knees, slowly, laboriously, as if his muscles weren't quite up to obeying his commands to move. Layla frowned. Possible hypothermia or concussion. She'd have to check him for frostbite, too. "Did you black out when you hit your head?"

"Not sure." He dragged himself up to stand on one foot, leaning heavily on her shoulder, shivering. "Don't think so. Fainted after, though. Twice. Hurt like hell."

Layla's lips twitched in amusement. Always the big strong ones who couldn't handle being injured. She'd met a kid in one of her schools in California, a rare friend named Pedro, who at fifteen was enormously tall and built like a truck. He'd passed out dissecting an earthworm in biology class, and told her later he even fainted when he got splinters. Her anxiety lessened. If Captain Commando caused her trouble, all she had to do was kick his ankle and he'd lose consciousness long enough for her to get to Jake.

"We're going to the house now." She took a step forward and he hopped to keep up with her, his weight heavy on her shoulder, then lighter when he landed. "If you feel faint, tell me and we'll stop so you can put your head down."

"'kay." The word came out clipped, and she knew the hopping wasn't helping his ankle feel any better. She hoped it wasn't broken, though at this point she was more concerned with his head injury.

Though why she should be concerned about anything involving this trespasser, other than getting him off her mountain as quickly as possible, she hadn't a clue. Once he was inside, with a storm like this, it could be days before she could kick him out. Her fear rose again, along with angry claustrophobia. Trapped in a cabin, having to be on her guard every second as his strength returned. She clenched her teeth. Whatever he was about, she wanted to know soon so she could stop having to worry and deal with it.

A particularly nasty blast of wind showered them with stinging snowflakes and knocked the man off balance midhop. He staggered against her; she turned and shot both arms around him to steady him. He rested his forehead on top of her hair; she felt his body shivering violently under her hands.

For one crazy second her senses registered that he smelled really, really good. Like pine and cold leather and...man. The next, much-saner second, she pulled back at the same time he did, both a little hurriedly, as if they'd been caught doing something naughty, and they resumed the painful hopping progress toward her cabin.

Once inside, Layla's gut tightened and panic again threatened to take over. She felt as though a flashing red light and whooping alarm should go off. *Intruder alert, intruder alert.* Even with Captain Commando in his weakened state, leaning on her to be able to move at all, he seemed once again large and threatening here in her private home.

She led him over to her bed and stared down at the wedding ring quilt her grandmother had started making when she was born, and which her grandfather had saved for her in this house. Somewhat childishly, she didn't want to look at him, as if not looking at him would somehow make him not be there. "Here. Lie down."

"No."

She did look at him then, a look of incredulity, taking in his ashen features and tottery stance. "Pardon me, but the way you look, either you lie down yourself or your body will take care of it for you."

"Don't want to take your bed." He bent his head forward, as if he was already losing the battle with unconsciousness.

"Oh, honestly. This isn't the time to play gallant." She yanked the covers down. "Get in."

"I can sleep on the fl—"

He landed on the bed with a grunt. Layla rolled her eyes. One quick shove and he'd toppled, probably on his way to passing out, anyway. He could certainly take her when his strength was up, but for now she had the upper hand.

"Turn over." She steeled herself. He was shivering even more violently now that he was lying down. She'd have to get him warm quickly, inspect his head, see if his ankle was broken, check fingers and toes for frostbite. She glanced at her watch. All before Baby got up and needed feeding.

The man turned over, moaning softly; his shaking increased. Layla ran to put two more logs on the fire, dumped pasta into the boiling water she'd completely forgotten was there, filled the kettle and set it on the stove, then dashed to her closet for a towel and back to her bed.

"I'm going to dry your hair and wrap this around your head so you don't lose more heat. I might hurt you."

"Yes. Okay." The words came out wobbly through his chattering teeth.

She rubbed his thick dark hair with the towel, pressing gently at the back where the lump was, then left the cloth wrapped around his head. Her fingers tested his nose and cheek, checking for signs of frostbite. His nose was shockingly cold, but not frozen; his cheeks were rough with stubble, but likewise not in danger.

"I'm going to take off your clothes."

"Yes." His voice sounded weak, altogether different from the smooth-talking customer she'd confronted in the woods.

She pulled his gloves off, felt his fingers. Still soft, the skin looked white but not swollen. Boots and socks were next; she tugged the one off his uninjured ankle, then as carefully and swiftly as she could, she unlaced and removed the other, wincing at his groan of pain. His ankle was swollen—taking off the boot had probably made it hurt more. She checked his feet, relieved to find his toes in the same shape as his fingers. "No frostbite. At least, not serious. Can you move your foot?"

He moved it forward and back and wiggled his toes. Layla gave a nod of satisfaction. "I'm going to assume your ankle is sprained because I have no way of knowing if it's broken. You'll probably find out when you try walking on it tomorrow."

"Okay."

Next. She tugged on his jacket; he helped feebly, moving his arms and raising his body as best he could despite the convulsive shivers. Sweater. Shirt. Undershirt. He submitted feebly, lying back on the bed as each article came off. Eyes closed, lashes dark on his too pale skin, he somehow managed to look handsome and masculine, sick as he was, with a pink towel on his head. She glanced at his chest, lean and muscled with the perfect amount of black hair, taking in the picture even while trying not to. The man looked like a freaking centerfold.

Pants. Her fingers worked quickly on the button and zipper. She felt the color rise in her cheeks. Get this over with fast. She pulled the wet jeans down his long

legs, eased them over his swollen ankle, then followed
suit with his briefs. She thrust a cushion under his
injured leg and practically threw the sheet on top of
him, following it with the thick wool blanket and quilt,
tucking all the layers tight around him.

Whew. Got that part over with. Time would tell how
bad a head injury he'd sustained. The rest of him was
in way too good shape for her peace of mind.

The kettle started to sing on the stove. She darted
from the bed, glad to be away from the stranger, needing time to compose herself. Baby stirred when she
passed the crib, but settled. Thank goodness. One
helpless individual at a time.

The shrill whistle decrescendoed into a tinny whimper when she turned off the flame. She measured dried
home-grown herbs into a pair of blue-green mugs
she'd made herself, filled them with boiling water,
drained her pasta and mixed in some olive oil to keep
it from clumping—who knew when she'd be able to
eat?—then got a jar of gorp she kept on hand to take
on hikes or when she needed quick energy.

Captain Commando would need the food and liquid
heat inside to warm up quickly. Layla just needed to
sip something calming, to try to come to terms with
having someone in her cabin around-the-clock. Someone mysterious and uninvited and unsettling, disturb-
ing her life and routine. She'd lived in this cabin for
eight years, on her own except for the week Baby's
father, Rick, had spent here.

Layla smiled wryly and shook her head. Another
lost, worse-for-wear hiker she'd taken in. But unlike
Captain Commando here, Rick had been a gentle,
thoughtful soul. They'd been drawn to each other im-

mediately and had passed three days as intimate lovers before he'd moved on.

"Where are you?"

She stiffened at the sound of the weak, hoarse voice, and went over to the bed carrying the mugs and food, her steps slow and reluctant. With another naked man in her bed, she didn't need bittersweet memories of that first time intruding.

"I'm here. Feeling warmer?"

"What day is it?" He moved restlessly, his shivering less severe. His color was pale, but not quite so deathly. His eyes, however, were still dull and slightly unfocused, nowhere near as intense as they'd been during their first encounter. Confusion could be a symptom of either hypothermia or serious concussion. With hypothermia, it would pass quickly as he warmed. If it stayed around, he could be in trouble.

"It's still today." She set the tea on the rough bedside table Rick had made for her, birch bark still on the legs, peeling in curling strips.

He turned those strange eyes on her. "I was looking for you."

"I'm right here."

"She said I had to find you. Your baby."

Layla frowned and helped him to sit up to drink. "Who said you had to find me?"

"Shana…"

Layla leaned closer, riveted on him. How lucid was he? She was certain no one who knew about Baby would have to get someone from Nebraska to help find her. "Who is Shana?"

He closed his eyes and lay still, shivering now only in quick startling bursts.

"You need to eat and drink something hot, to warm up."

Layla nudged him, repeating the words until he opened his eyes and accepted some of the snack mix from her hand. Sleep was not a good idea until she was sure his body temperature was back to normal. He chewed, swallowed and tried a few sips of tea from the cup she held for him. Then more tea. More food. Again. And again. His shivering gradually became less spastic; he was probably out of danger from the cold. She'd just need to stay alert for signs of brain injury.

"Who is Shana?"

"Sister. I had to help him find you. Because...the baby."

Layla fed him more snack and held the cup for him again. Help *him* find her? Was he talking about Rick? Was it possible Rick had counted the months after their idyllic tryst and wanted to know if he'd left her with a child? One night the condom had broken or ripped or fallen off or something—she couldn't claim to be a birth control expert. Apparently that had been all it had taken.

He'd worried about leaving her pregnant, had said in his thoughtful, absentminded way that she would have so little support up here to raise a child. He'd also made it clear, not unkindly, that he had no money or time or desire to help, though of course he would if it came to that. She didn't blame him for feeling that way. In fact, she entirely understood.

So she'd lied and said there was no way she could get pregnant that week. That it was entirely the wrong time in her cycle. Because as fond as she was of him, she didn't want him coming back out of some sense of duty to check on her, didn't want to be tied to anyone, especially someone who didn't want the burden of a child out of wedlock.

Even when she found out she was going to have a baby, she hadn't tried to find him; she'd even briefly considered not going through with the pregnancy. What did she know about motherhood? With rare exceptions, her own mother had been a walking guidebook on how not to be a parent. What kind of life could she offer a child?

In the end she'd simply been unable to terminate the pregnancy. It had seemed an act of God that such an unlikely set of circumstances had left her with a child.

But if that theory were true, if Rick wanted to know for sure, if he hadn't believed her when she'd said such a thing wasn't possible, why hadn't he come himself?

"Did Rick send you to find out if I had a baby?"

He opened his eyes and stared blankly, then frowned.

Layla felt a surge of frustration and tamped it down. Not his fault he wasn't entirely coherent. "Did Rick send you?"

"Find you. Find the baby." He shook his head, closed his eyes again.

Layla gripped the mug in her hands. What the hell was going on? Was this Shana person Rick's girlfriend? Fiancée? Was Rick making sure he had no stray kids in the world before he married? Very much like him to be so honorable. But she didn't want him to know, didn't want him or anyone connected to him to come here. Maybe she'd have to lie again, tell this man that the baby wasn't Rick's. That she had a steady stream of lost hikers coming through, one every quarter, seducing her and breaking their condoms.

This guy might buy it, but Rick never would. They'd had a special bond and had recognized each other as nearly kindred spirits.

She slumped off her knees onto her butt on the chilly plank floor, then just as quickly straightened again. No point getting worked up over something that was pure conjecture. The stranger probably had no idea what he was saying. She'd make sure he was okay, that he got warm before he slept, then she'd get the real story from him in the morning.

After most of the tea was gone, he'd eaten a decent amount and his shivering stopped, she went to find a wrap for his ankle. Once Captain Commando was settled, she could waken Baby for a feeding and some play time. It was only eight, but she was pretty damn tired herself and didn't relish the idea of Baby waking at 4:00 a.m., raring to start her day. Add to that the fact that she herself wouldn't sleep well, knowing there was a strange man in the cabin.

Among the neat stockpile of medicines, herbs and Band-Aids, she found the elastic bandage she'd bought her first summer here, before she'd had her mountain legs, when she'd sprained her own ankle after leaping onto untested ground in a fit of exuberance. It had been a sobering experience to be injured when she was so alone. She'd learned a hell of a lot about safety and independence in the past eight years.

The bandage went on fairly smoothly; the stranger groaned once or twice, then drifted back into what seemed like a natural sleep. Layla moved to the head of the bed and felt his forehead. Warm. Good. She carefully removed the towel, so his hair could dry thoroughly. His head would probably hurt like hell in the morning, but with any luck he would be spared a bad concussion and the accompanying brain swelling.

Baby stirred, whimpered, then cried softly. Layla hurried over to the crib and picked her up before her noise woke the captain. Enough excitement for one day. She'd spend some time with Baby, sing her the songs she loved—"Eensy Weensy Spider" and "Baby's Workin' on a Railroad"—let her test out some toys and textures, then Layla would eat her cold pasta hours after she usually had it, and get some sleep.

She had a feeling she was going to need it.

BRETT WOKE TO THE SURREAL experience of having no idea where he was. It was dark, nighttime, he could tell that. He felt as though he'd been asleep only a few hours. Blinking cautiously at the unfamiliar vaulted pine ceiling, lit with a steady yellow glow, he cautiously turned his head, wincing when someone simultaneously ground his scalp with sandpaper while shooting several bullets past his eyes.

He pulled up his legs to turn onto his side and had the added pleasure of someone dropping an anvil on his ankle.

Obviously he had not had a good evening.

He could hear a storm raging outside, the cabin walls buffeted by wind; inside he could hear the comforting crackle of a fire and the soft, soothing sound of a woman humming. He tried to focus his uncooperative eyes and finally managed. Layla. Sitting across the room in a rocking chair, nursing her baby, firelight glinting off her straight blond hair. In direct contrast to the gun-toting mama he'd first encountered, she looked vulnerable and feminine, cradling her child, intent on the small face sucking at her breast.

Everything came back. His fall in the woods—a bit fuzzy after that—then seeing her, stopping to rest on his way in and feeling her slender arms around him, the surprise of the iron in their strength, the feel of her hair under his cheek. Coming inside to warmth, blankets, food, comfort, tea.

Tea.

Lots of tea.

Damn.

He lifted his hands out of the blankets and ran them over his face. There was no way he could make it outside by himself. Hell, he wasn't even sure he could sit up by himself. He lifted up onto his elbows, testing. The room swirled for a few seconds, then made an unconvincing stab at settling back into its usual stability. His brain felt like a gyroscope.

A sound that took him straight back to his rude adolescent days startled him. He turned, eyebrows raised, to find Layla holding the baby to her shoulder, patting the tiny back, watching him warily.

"She says excuse me."

He dipped his head and gave a silent whistle, then wished he hadn't when the anvil-dropper moved from his ankle to his skull. "She'll go far."

Layla either didn't find that funny or had been formed without a sense of humor because her expression didn't change. She continued to regard him with a strange mixture of hostility and curiosity, the way he imagined a bear would examine a hiker while deciding whether to walk away or to begin the mauling and maiming.

"How are you feeling?" She got out of the rocker

in a graceful movement and walked toward him.
"Does your head hurt?"

"Like mad."

She nodded and stopped a few feet away, both arms
wrapped around her child, though from the look on
her face, he couldn't tell if she was offering protection
or accepting it. "Do you need anything to drink?"

"*No.*" The word came out too loud in the sleepy
cabin interior and her baby jumped, whimpered, then
settled her head back on her mom's shoulder.

Layla lifted an eyebrow. "Okay."

Brett put his hands to his temples. He'd faced guns,
death threats, hostile gangs and drug-crazed teenagers,
yet was intimidated as hell having to ask this strange
hermit girl to help him use the bathroom.

"I need to go." He felt like a three-year-old asking
his mom for permission. The dependency irritated him.
She irritated him. Right now with his head on fire and
his ankle throbbing, everything irritated him.

"You're not going anywhere in that condition."

He gritted his teeth. "No. I need to *go.*"

"Oh." Layla nodded as if his statement was the
most natural thing in the world, which now that he
thought about it, it probably was. She put the baby in
an infant seat and rummaged on a high shelf built into
the walls and covered with a bright length of fabric.

"Here." She walked back toward him, carrying a
pot with a lid.

He felt his face flame. "You want me to use your
cookware?"

That eyebrow lifted again in the how-stupid-do-you-
think-I-am expression he was starting to hate. "It's a
chamber pot."

Brett gritted his teeth. Of course it was a chamber

pot. And he was going to have to use it in front of her and expect her to empty it. He'd rather hold it until he exploded.

She came to the side of the bed and put it on the floor. "Need help standing?"

A huge resounding macho "No way" rose to his lips before he realized that, in fact, he did, and bit it back. His resentment increased. No doubt if Ms. Layla was in possession of a sense of humor, buried deep somewhere, she was finding this all very amusing. "Help would be good."

She nodded and approached him without hesitation, as if she helped strange men urinate every day, then sat on the bed next to him and pulled his arm around her shoulders.

He pushed off the covers and moved to stand, wincing at the pain in his ankle and at the same moment realizing something he hadn't thought of before.

"I'm naked."

The eyebrow lifted. He felt like growling, but it would make his head hurt worse, if such a thing were possible.

"I know. I got you that way."

Okay. Deep breath. He could only be more humiliated if he let on how humiliated he was.

He stood, not letting the pain show, and used the damn chamber pot with this astonishingly strong woman supporting him, her face turned half away from the miserable damn sight of him peeing in a glorified bucket in a tiny damn female cabin on the top of a damn mountain during a damn blizzard.

As the last of the liquid was draining from his body, he began to realize that the last of the blood was also draining from his head.

"Damn" would no longer do as an adjective. Things were starting to get serious. The cabin danced and sparked in front of his eyes. He had to piss in front of this woman, but he'd be way more than damned if he was going to faint in front of her.

The room grew dim. *Hang on, Brett.* Mercifully he finished.

"All set?"

Her voice seemed far away; his answering assent rang thunderously in his own ears. He turned, clammy and pale, and heard her gasp.

"Lie down." Her order came, urgent and echoey, just as he took the last step to the bed and fell, vaguely aware she'd be trapped underneath him.

CHAPTER FIVE

TERRIFIC.

Layla glared at the ceiling over Brett's shoulder. The perfect ironic illustration of how she felt with this man in her house. Trapped. Currently under roughly two hundred pounds of muscular male.

Make that naked muscular male.

She gave a sharp wiggle and jabbed his hard shoulder with her hand. "Wake up."

He answered with a groan of abject misery that made her roll her eyes. Any grown man who knew he was going to faint—he *must* have known—who didn't put his head down to avoid it was a macho ass.

She pushed at his shoulder again, but he lay like a dead weight on her. "Get off me."

Her hand slid down his shoulder and latched onto a biceps, bulging, even in a relaxed state. She shook his arm and he flexed it, turning the biceps into a boulder under her fingers.

The feel of the hard muscle turned her exasperation into alarm, tinged with another kind of awareness she wasn't going to acknowledge to save her life. He might be concussed and woozy, but in their current situation, she was the one who was helpless.

She wriggled in sudden panic, desperately trying to get him off her.

Strong hands grabbed her shoulders. "Hold still. You're killing me."

"Get *off*."

He lifted his head and scowled down at her. "I'm trying. Give me a break here."

"Give *you* a break. You're lying on top of me."

"I am well aware of that."

Something in his voice made her swallow and hold still. "You're crushing me."

"I can't—" His eyes narrowed, he looked at her as if her face had suddenly come clearly into focus.

Layla struggled to control her breathing and let out a small helpless gasp she hated herself for.

Immediately he rolled off her, the effort clearly costing him. "I'm sorry. I needed a second to regroup. I didn't mean to scare you."

Layla shot off the bed and stood over him, hands clenched into involuntary fists at her side. "You didn't scare me."

She could hear the residual fear in her voice.

"Good."

She knew he didn't believe her. Why should he, when the truth of it was so obvious? But she gave him grudging credit for sparing her pride at least, and was glad she'd held back her scorn for not telling her that he was going to faint.

He moved back under the covers and closed his eyes. She resisted the urge to tuck the blankets in more firmly around him, settling instead for lifting them and replacing the pillow under his ankle.

"Thanks." He opened his eyes and gave her a brief smile, then closed them again, obviously exhausted.

She cleaned the chamber pot and replaced it by his bed, though from his barely concealed mortification earlier, she'd guess he'd rather take a slow cruise through hell than use it again.

She changed into sweats, not wanting to be caught dead waking up in the same room with him tomorrow in her usual flannel nightgown, checked on Baby one last time and made up the couch with sheets and an unzipped sleeping bag for a blanket. That done, she blew out the lamp and held still, standing in the quiet cabin, listening to the storm outside and the even, heavy breathing coming from her bed on the other side of the room. She grabbed the sleeping bag and turned it back to crawl in. A quiet groan stopped her.

For another long second she hovered, willing her body to get into her makeshift bed and rest.

But the strange pull was too strong. She stole across the cabin floor and up to her bed, just checking on him, just making sure he was okay, that his head injury wasn't serious. She actually ought to waken him; one of the signs of serious concussion was an inability to wake from sleep.

She put out her hand, touched the smooth skin of his shoulder, which had emerged from the thick layer of blankets she had tucked over him.

"Can you wake up?"

He didn't move, except to furrow his brow slightly. She leaned forward over him, touched his shoulder more firmly.

"Hello?" She spoke louder this time. "Can you—"

His arm shot out of the covers; he grabbed her wrist with incredible force, his eyes unnaturally wide.

Layla let out a short scream and tried to yank her arm back. Even in his weakened state, she might as well have been trying to break free of an iron cuff.

"Let go."

He blinked and blinked again, then released her abruptly, putting his hand to his head. "Layla. What the hell are you doing sneaking up on me?"

"I wasn't sneaking. I was trying to wake you."

"I'm awake." He covered his face with his hands as if the dim glow of the firelight hurt his eyes. "What the hell is it?"

"Nothing."

"*Nothing?* This was just an exercise in jollity? Scare the shit out of the stranger and see what he does?"

She gritted her teeth, extremely glad she hadn't picked nursing as a career. Men were such charmers when they didn't feel well. "You might have a concussion. I was trying to wake you to make sure I could."

"You could."

"Obviously." She turned to walk away and jerked back when he grabbed hold of her wrist again. "Will you stop doing that?"

"I'm…sorry." He said the word as if it was a brand new one he was trying out. "I'm not at my best."

"It's okay." She gave a gentle tug against the hand holding her, but he either didn't notice or didn't want to let go.

"I understand you needed to see if I could wake up. It was a smart thing to do."

"Thanks." She gave a less gentle tug, but he still held on. Why wouldn't he let her go? "Did you need anything more? Tea or something? Water? Food?"

"No."

"Then can you let go of me, please?"

"Layla."

Her stomach started to feel uneasy. Not entirely in

an unpleasant way, either, which was the last thing she needed. "What?"

"You probably saved my life."

"Probably." She hunched her shoulders, wanting to avoid a gooey gratitude scene at all costs. "It's no big deal. You would have done the same if you'd come across me in your backyard."

"True." He cleared his throat. She had an instinctive feeling that he was usually the one doing the saving and that this was an unnatural and not entirely welcome thing for him to be on the receiving end. "But thanks just the same."

He dropped her hand and closed his eyes, as if the ordeal of being grateful had sapped the last of his strength.

"You're welcome." She spoke gently, then had to push away a strange, nearly tender feeling before it started to take her over. She didn't know why he was here. Just because he was gorgeous and had managed to be polite for a few sentences didn't mean she should go soft or let down an iota of her guard.

Still, she lingered for a few seconds, tucking the covers back around him, nodding when he opened his eyes to smile at her, before she moved back to her couch, crawled in and lay there, wondering for way too long what kind of change Captain Commando would bring to her life.

HE WAS ON TOP of her again, his naked weight pressing her into the bed. She struggled to be free and her struggling turned him on, made his eyes half close, his mouth half open in overwhelming pleasure. She felt herself respond, felt the needy ache between her legs, and started pushing back against him for her own self-

*ish pleasure. He kissed her, his mouth warm and pos-
sessive, then he pulled back and smiled, his eyes a
deep brown that slowly, horribly, turned into snake-
yellow. His tongue flickered out, red and forked; his
smooth male skin grew scales. He slithered off her,
over to Baby's crib; lifted the child and took her away
on his reptilian back while Layla fought vainly to rise
out of a bed that was slowly, cruelly, drowning her in
its softness.*

Layla woke with a start on the couch, her terrified
whimpers still audible on the edge of her consciousness. She rolled her eyes, the uneasy creepy feeling
lingering from the dream, and allowed herself to find
it amusing while she calmed her breathing and her
heartbeat. Freud would have a field day with that one.
A naked guy who turned into a snake? Come on.

The absurdity made her smile, but did nothing to
banish her uneasiness. On impulse, she got off the
couch and tiptoed across the chilly room to Baby's
crib, forcing herself not to glance at the man sleeping
in her bed. Her instinct told her it was around five,
close to the time Baby usually called to her for breakfast. Since she couldn't start a fire or any other part
of her morning routine for fear of waking the stranger
before she was ready to deal with him—not that she
was sure she'd ever be ready—she'd wake Baby, bring
her to bed, and feed her.

They'd both enjoy the comfort, and maybe they
could sleep some more until Captain Commando decided to wake up and allow them to start their day.

She lifted Baby out, cuddled her to her own warmth,
hurried back into bed and fit the always-eager mouth
onto her breast. Gradually the sensation of residual
creepiness brought on by the dream was replaced by

the closeness and shared warmth between her and her child.

Regardless of what this man would mean to her life, regardless of the news he brought, this was real, this was important, and this wouldn't ever change.

SHE WOKE, for the second time that morning, to find Baby still in her couch bed. She blinked and looked around the cabin, taking in the light and the feel of her surroundings. It must be close to seven. Layla couldn't remember the last time she'd woken so late. Seemed a shocking luxury. She sat up carefully and stretched her arms over her head, deliberately resisting the urge to turn to see if Captain Commando was awake.

"Good morning." His deep voice made her jump. Welcome to Day One of "A Stranger in Her Home."

She was going to hate it.

"Good morning."

She turned to look at him, trying to pretend it wasn't unbearably and inappropriately intimate to be waking up in the same room together. He'd obviously spent a good night after he'd gone back to sleep; his color was better and his eyes had stopped looking as if it was a tremendous effort to focus. "You look a hell of a lot better."

"That bad, was I?" He grinned, as if the idea of him being anything but strong and in control was ludicrous.

"You don't remember?"

He grinned wider. "I remember some things."

For no logical reason, except maybe the touch of mischief in his eyes, she had a fleeting conviction that he was thinking about having fainted on top of her.

She was going to get his clothes for him. Now.

She pushed back the sleeping bag and carefully returned Baby to her crib, sleeping bag and all, breathing a sigh of relief when the child didn't wake missing her warmth. A glance at the window told her the damn snow was still coming down hard. If Captain Commando's truck was stuck, as he'd said yesterday, there would be no chance of getting him a tow in this weather. He'd be here forever, underfoot, to be served, nursed, accommodated...

She moved toward the woodstove, where she'd hung his pants and shirt to dry, hurriedly built a fire, then grabbed the clothes, marched over to him and shoved them at his naked chest.

"Here. I'm going out. Please check on the baby once in a while to make sure she doesn't get swallowed by the sleeping bag."

She grabbed clothes of her own, zipped on her parka, stomped on her boots and went outside into the storm to use the outhouse and get dressed in freezing-cold peace. If pushed, she'd admit that it eased her mind somewhat to have someone on guard for Baby while she had to be out of the cabin. Otherwise, this storm couldn't end soon enough.

By the time she got back, the cabin was noticeably warmer and the stranger was noticeably clothed. These were good things. The bad news was that dressed and looking healthier, sitting on her bed, he took up half the cabin. It wasn't only his physical size; that aura of confidence she'd noticed in the woods by the driveway was back, filling up the space and leaving less room for her.

"I'm Brett Devlin." He extended his hand. "I think we skipped the hi-my-name-is, damn-glad-to-meet-you part and went straight to the shooting and blizzard and life-threatening injury.''

Layla's lips twitched in response to his grin, even as part of her wished she didn't have to know his name. Keeping him anonymous had meant distance she needed—especially while he was naked. But he had clothes on now, and of course it wasn't realistic to think they could live together for a few days without using names. Though she kind of liked Captain Commando.

''Hi.'' She stood there, feeling stupid and awkward, wanting to ask him again why he was here, now that lucidity had apparently returned to him, but his introduction had made the intimacy unbearable; she needed to escape into her morning routine.

''So…how is your head?'' She started edging toward the kitchen, annoyed when he followed her movement with an amused look, as if he knew why she was uncomfortable.

''Feels like hell, but I'll survive.''

''Are you hungry?''

He nodded sheepishly. ''I know you didn't plan on having a houseguest. I appreciate this.''

''Don't worry about it.'' She fled to her tiny kitchen area and set about making her usual morning breakfast of multigrain porridge cooked with raisins and dried apricots, double the portion and then some. She had a healthy appetite, especially now that she was breastfeeding, and she had a feeling that after an injury and most of yesterday without food, he could eat an elephant under the table.

While the porridge simmered, she checked on Baby, smoothing the blond downy hair.

''What's your child's name?''

The voice made her jump. She turned her head slightly to acknowledge the question, but without looking at him. "I call her…her name is Phoebe."

No way was she telling a stranger that she couldn't bring herself to use the child's name.

"How old is she?"

"Nearly two months."

"Must be a lot of work caring for an infant in a place like this."

Layla bristled. From what she heard, it was a lot of work caring for an infant in any place. "I manage."

"Obviously."

He must have gotten up because she heard his uneven shuffle coming toward her.

She shrank away from his enormous presence as he stood next to her, squinting down at the child as if his eyes wouldn't quite focus on their own yet.

"She's very cute." He said the words as if he knew cooing was required, but he was supremely uncomfortable providing any.

"Thanks."

Layla moved away from him to stir the porridge. She'd go nuts having to make small talk all day. Rick had been the strong silent type; they'd done very little talking. Neither had felt it necessary, and they'd still managed to get a strong sense of each other.

"Can I help?" He limped after her toward the kitchen.

She looked pointedly at his ankle. Nice of him to offer, she guessed, but grounding herself in her usual set of morning tasks was comforting. Having him hovering around, awaiting instructions, would frazzle her even more. "I can do it, thanks."

"Okay. I'll make a trip outside."

"Need any help?" The words came out grudging and insincere. She was nearly ashamed of herself.

His chuckle turned his tough, handsome face boyish. "Well, gee. If you're *that* anxious to..."

She gave a small embarrassed smile, not meeting his eyes, and shrugged, wanting to belt him for sarcasm, though she probably deserved it.

"I have a walking stick that might help." She pointed to it in the corner next to the door.

"Thanks." He limped over and retrieved it. The stick was too short, but he gamely managed to get himself out into the blowing snow. She'd have to find him a larger one next time she was outside.

Ten minutes later she had breakfast on the table, tea ready in large thick blue mugs and the hot cereal in white bowls with a blue lupin pattern, and was scowling at the table. Intimate breakfast for two, sitting opposite each other as if they were lovers.

She'd rather snack on nails, even though her stomach was growling for food, two hours later than she usually ate it.

She went over to the crib, lifted Baby out, awake or not, and took her seat in the rocker to feed her, so that when Brett returned, he'd find her busy and could eat his damn breakfast by his damn self.

Except that when he came in, he took off his snowy hiking boots rather painfully and settled himself near her on the cedar chest her great-grandparents had gotten as a wedding present.

"Your breakfast is ready." She wanted to scream at him to leave her alone.

"I see that. It looks delicious."

Baby's eyes widened at the unfamiliar voice. She

suddenly let go of Layla's breast, leaving her nipple open for viewing.

"You go ahead." She shoved Baby's mouth back into place, commanding herself not to blush. "I'm giving Ba-Phoebe hers."

"It looks delicious, too."

Layla shot him the look she used on tormentors at various schools, where she imagined her glare had the power to cook them into crispy bully strips. "Go ahead and eat."

He smiled, his eyes flicking up to hers from where they'd apparently been glued to Baby's head at her breast. "I can wait."

Her body tensed; she felt herself flushing with anger and a strange tension. Baby sensed the change and pulled back again with a cry.

"Shh, Baby, it's okay." She offered the breast again. "Please. Go. Eat."

He didn't move, the jerk; she could see out of her peripheral vision that he was still watching her.

"I'm curious."

"*What.*" She finally looked up.

He raised two innocent-as-pie eyebrows, which put her even more on guard. "Are you going to be this hostile the entire time I'm here?"

"Absolutely." The word burst out of her. She met his eyes defiantly, expecting exasperation, and found herself instead looking at a slowly spreading smile. Worse, she felt her own mouth wanting to spread into an answering one.

He leaned forward in his chair, forearms resting across his thighs so that the distance between them was shortened, not by much, but enough to make whatever he was about to say seem far too intimate.

She felt the flush rise again in her face. Once more, he had her defenseless, sitting here with her naked breast out, a child in her arms. She glanced longingly at Jake.

"Look, I know I'm not your dream companion for the next day or two."

Layla jerked her head toward the snowy window. "Or three."

"Or three." He nodded. "I want you to know that I feel awkward about this and I'm sorry."

Her blush deepened. She had no idea what to do with this charming apology except to accept it graciously. In doing so, she lost her primary weapon against him, that of put-upon outrage. She searched frantically for another, the instinct of self-protection strong. Against what, she still wasn't sure, which bothered her almost more than being defenseless.

"Why are you here?" The words came out more accusation than question.

He didn't blink, didn't seem surprised, and didn't answer.

Layla's heart began a slow powerful thud; Baby stopped sucking and gazed at her as if she was wondering what in the world had turned her mom into a dragon lady. "Answer me."

He rose and strolled over to the table, picked up a mug and took a sip of tea, glancing at the blue-green speckled glaze. "I was sent here to find you. And Phoebe."

"Who sent you?"

"I think it's better you don't know just yet."

Layla hoisted Baby to her shoulder and began rhythmic patting; Baby's head bounced against her and she gentled her touch.

"What kind of hyper-mysterious bull is that? 'It's better you don't know.'" She snorted and continued thumping Baby's back. "You'd damn well better tell me. I have a right to know."

"Yes. You do." He put the mug down, toying with the handle in the way he did everything, as if even his idle movements had great purpose and importance. "Just not right now."

"When?"

"Soon enough."

"Oh, honestly. You sound like a B-movie actor. 'Soon enough.'"

He lifted his eyes from contemplation of her table to contemplation of her. "I know it sounds strange. I'll have to ask you to trust me that it's best that way."

"I have exactly zero reasons to trust you."

"True." He sat and started eating. "This is delicious. Thank you."

Layla tightened her lips, still patting Baby desperately, as if getting the child to burp would release all of the tension in the room. "Last night you said something about your sister named Shana and helping some man find me. What were you talking about?"

"I was delirious."

She wasn't remotely convinced, but the calm, level stare he directed at her before he went back to his meal told her loud and clear that she wasn't getting anything more out of him until his "soon enough" arrived, whenever the hell that would be.

Why wouldn't he tell her now? Was he waiting for something or someone? He'd seemed perfectly happy to chat when he'd first showed up. What had changed except the storm and his injury?

"Why did you leave and come back?"

"I didn't want to get my balls shot off." He lifted a spoonful of porridge to his mouth, blew on it and swallowed, then dug in again. "Pretty reasonable, I think. I was also thinking I'd give you a chance to cool off and get curious, maybe make you more receptive. But when I heard about the storm, I realized I could get stuck waiting three days in town before I could get back up here. Ironic, considering I'm stuck here now."

"So why not tell me now? Are you afraid of what I'll do?" Her voice sounded scared, angry, bitter, like some other woman's voice. She didn't want to bring up her theory about Rick wanting to find her, didn't want to share him with this stranger in case she was wrong.

"Layla." He looked at her over his next spoonful of porridge, like a teacher reproaching an impatient child.

She rolled her eyes. "'Soon enough.' You're not telling me a damn thing now. I'm supposed to sit here for God knows how long and wait to find out if you're going to tell me I inherited six million dollars, or that I'm wanted for a crime I didn't commit, or that my house is being repossessed for some reason..."

His brow furrowed. He stopped eating. "I didn't mean it to work out like that."

"Well, it did."

He pushed impatiently away from the table. "We're only going to talk ourselves in circles here. It's a complicated issue. You won't lose your house, you're not implicated in any crime. And, unfortunately, you also haven't inherited six million, at least not as far as I know. Can we drop it? We have two or three days here together—we might as well try to make them as pleasant as possible.''

She leaned her head back sharply and banged it on the top of the rocker, still patting Baby furiously. Closing her eyes, she counted to ten, though infinity still wouldn't be enough to calm her down. She sensed he wasn't one to crack under pressure, that she could nag and threaten and beg and plead, but even Jake wouldn't help.

After she'd taken all this trouble to bring Brett in and nurse him back to health, he'd never believe now that she was capable of shooting him. Quite possibly he did think he had some good reason for putting off telling her, though she doubted she'd agree. More likely he was waiting until the snow stopped, so he could dump bad news on her and escape quickly.

"Okay. I'll drop it.''

"And one more thing.''

"What?" She practically growled the word.

"If you keep thumping the kid like that, her head is going to pop off.''

Layla stopped thumping. The second her hand stilled, Baby came up with one of her patented earth-shaking belches.

"Impressive.'' He lifted and lowered his dark brows. "She'll get a lot of dates in junior high.''

Layla glared at him to hide an absurd giggle, stood, and stalked to the changing table, where she changed Baby with ferocious speed. The day loomed ahead, endless, tense and exhausting.

She was damn sure it was going to be the longest of her life.

BRETT STRETCHED HIS LEGS under the table and drained the last of another mug of tea, longing for a triple espresso. This had to have been one of the longest days of his life. And it wasn't even dinnertime yet. Layla hadn't resorted to the shotgun again, but she'd done everything else possible to make him feel unwelcome. He'd tried friendly chatter, but that had fallen flat. Fine by him. He wasn't an innate chatterer. Then he'd tried to help her around the house. But apparently nothing could be done correctly unless she did it.

The worst was the lunch episode. He'd practically had to wrestle her to get her to let him make lunch. Then he'd discovered she had the same thing for lunch every day at the exact same time. Peanut butter and jelly at noon.

Fine. He liked a good peanut-butter sandwich himself. But he discovered he made his the wrong way. His amazement had given way to amusement, which had sauntered right on into annoyance. The peanut butter had to go on both pieces of bread, spread thin, smooth on one side, chunky on the other. Then jelly, just on the creamy side. Then cut the bread on the diagonal into quarters.

At one point he'd turned and interrupted her with a frankly incredulous stare. To her credit, she'd bitten off her list of instructions, looked startled, and then blushed.

So maybe he was weird, too, living alone so long. He liked his chunky peanut butter on one piece, jelly on the other, sandwich cut in two vertically. If someone came into his house and made it another way, maybe he'd speak up, too.

But he doubted it.

Finally, about an hour ago, when Phoebe went down

for a nap, Layla had fled to her pottery wheel in a shed out back, leaving him here with the baby, in utter terror in case it woke up. He had a feeling Layla had reached her limit concerning him.

Well, he could probably say the same about her. Except that she did intrigue him. What could possibly induce a beautiful, vibrant young woman to lock herself away in this tiny cabin in the middle of nowhere? To shoot at him one minute and save his life the next? For one weird moment he wished they didn't have this bad news hanging over them. Wished he could just get into her head to find out what made her tick. People were his specialty, and she didn't fit any of the molds he'd encountered previously.

He stood abruptly, wincing when his head gave a nasty throb for punishment, and went over to the sink to put away the dishes she'd miraculously allowed him to let air-dry after lunch instead of wiping immediately. One thing he'd have to admit, she was a talented artist. The plates were awash in shapes and shades of orange, red and yellow, like eating off a sunrise. There was a strange sense of passion about them, though he felt ludicrous assigning passion to plates. The mugs, in contrast, were cool blues and greens, the bowls flowery and feminine. All parts of the same person?

He shrugged. It was unlike him to be so fanciful. They were plates. Nice ones. Made by a proud, stubborn wacko woman.

And speaking of stubborn women, he'd better call Shana while he had the chance. She'd be dying to find out how things were going. Not that he had anything to tell her. In fact it was tempting to put off the call until the time was right to tell Layla the truth about her natural daughter. But he could practically sense

Shana's tension from here, and since she'd last left him with his truck off the road, she'd be happy to hear that he'd made it back up to the cabin—and that his truck was off the road once again.

He put the last dish away and looked around—God forbid he leave anything out of place—got his satellite phone and dialed, glancing guiltily out the window for signs of Layla coming back.

"Shana, it's Brett."

"Brett! Oh, my gosh, I've been a wreck. *Keith, it's Brett.*" Her voice went distant as she called out to her boyfriend. "So what's going on? Did you go back? Did you tell her? How did she take it? Does she want to see her baby? Will she let Bruce Lehr adopt his niece?"

Brett held up his hand as if she could see him trying to stop her torrent of words. "Whoa, Shana, slow down."

"Okay, okay, I'm listening. Tell me."

He took a deep breath and told her the story, making light of his injuries so she wouldn't insist on a rescue helicopter.

"So I'm stuck here…" He lifted his arm and let it slap down onto his thigh.

"Oh, but, Brett, that's perfect!"

He narrowed his eyes. That wasn't the word he'd use. "Perfect exactly how?"

"Because now you can be there for her for a couple of days while she adjusts to the news. How did she take it?"

His stomach tensed. Shana always managed to make him feel guilty for who he was. "I haven't told her."

"You haven't *told* her?"

"No. I haven't told her, which is why I just said,

'I haven't told her.''' He gritted his teeth. Something about Shana's earnest integrity brought out the jerk in him.

"But today, right? Maybe after dinner when the baby's asleep?"

"Shana. My job was to find this woman. I am telling her the news as a favor to you. Staying around and acting as her personal therapist is not in my job description."

"Oh, Brett."

Her mournful tone made him press his lips together so tightly they hurt. Their mom had perfected that tone. Only, she'd used it whenever something hadn't pleased her personally. Shana used it on behalf of others.

"Don't 'Oh, Brett' me, young lady." He used his "Father Knows Best" voice and made her laugh.

"I'm sorry. It's just that you work so damn hard at being an ass, and I wonder why sometimes."

He shook his head, chuckling without humor. "I know, I know. Your big brother should be worthy of worship. Sorry to disappoint you."

"I just don't understand what you've got against the human race."

"The human race is what I've got against the human race."

Shana groaned in exasperation. "Just think how it would feel if you were her."

"If I were her, I wouldn't want some stranger hanging around while I was grieving over something that was none of his damn business."

"Oh, Brett."

He rolled his eyes. "I'll tell her right before I leave,

Shana. Believe me, she doesn't need me. This woman needs no one. She's tough as they come.''

"No one's that tough."

"This woman is."

The line went silent for a few seconds, which always got his guard up. Shana was concocting something. "You admire her."

"Yes. I do."

More silence. He put his hand to his forehead. This was going to be good.

"Is there something going on between you two?"

"Oh, for God's sake, Shana."

"Sorry, sorry, just curious. You don't sound quite like yourself."

"I practically had my brains bashed out, I sprained my ankle, I'm trapped for three days with this woman whose life I've been sent to disrupt—no, I don't exactly feel like myself."

He went to the window, pulled back the curtain and stared out at the swirling snow. The trouble was, he couldn't tell how much of his predicament was circumstance and how much of it was Layla.

He pictured her, proud and aggressive and scared behind the shotgun in her worn parka, strong and practical helping him, nurturing and feminine while breastfeeding her child in a rocker, looking for all the world as though she should be in some ruffly type of dress.

Layla hadn't exactly endeared herself to him, but, he'd admit, the picture of her crumpled here alone with her shock and grief after he left wasn't appealing.

He pushed his hand through his hair and blew out a sigh of frustration. He couldn't see another way around it. What help would he be to her here? She didn't know him, didn't trust him. A woman like her would want to be alone.

He'd wait. The storm would end, the plows would come. He'd know the right moment. He'd go on instinct.

In the meantime he'd concentrate on getting stronger and avoiding her as much as possible.

"Okay, I'm sorry." His sister's voice was contrite and he felt like a jerk. Again.

"Don't worry about it, Shana. This whole situation is stressful."

"I had a talk with Jaron Dorsey this morning, about the case."

"What's the latest?"

"Well, first off, according to the hospital records in Glacier, the baby Layla has is named Alycia Lehr. Her parents were Patty and Jim. Oh! And Jaron has met Jim's brother, Bruce. The one who wants to adopt Alycia."

"And?" Brett felt a strange hostile tension in his body. This guy could be a saint, no doubt he had every right to his niece, but it still bugged Brett that Bruce Lehr was in essence taking Layla's baby away. "What did Jaron report?"

"All sounds good. Bruce moved back to live in Seattle, his hometown, with his fiancée Anne, now his wife, after living in France for several years. When he couldn't locate his brother, he contacted the Seattle police. He's educated, wealthy, an apparently upright and terrific citizen, and he and his wife can't have children of their own. So this is a godsend to them."

Brett tightened his jaw. *Yeah, to them.* "Jaron have any more on why Jim and Patty Lehr thought it was a good idea to switch babies with someone else?"

She gave a sigh closer to a groan. "Apparently they had a previous baby die of a severe form of Downs. The police think maybe they switched Alycia because they were afraid of the same thing happening again."

He frowned incredulously. "This baby is perfect."

"I know, that's the strange thing. But babies aren't perfect when they're born. Maybe the Lehrs thought…" She made a sound of frustration. "Well, we'll never know what they thought. Both babies were born in the ER that night instead of Labor and Delivery, so the ID bracelets were delayed. I guess the Lehrs saw an opportunity, maybe they just panicked. I don't know. It's ugly all around."

"That's for sure." Damn selfish couple, ditching a child they thought might be ill on someone else. On Layla.

"Apparently in the hospital after the car accident, before she died herself, Patty Lehr kept insisting her baby was dying. The staff kept checking the baby that was in the car with her, obviously thinking it was hers, and reassuring her, but she stuck to the story."

"God, what a waste."

His sister was silent for too long. He was on his guard instantly.

"Um…Brett?"

"What?"

"Are you actually horrified by this story? Does the fact that these people did something thoughtless and stupid actually upset you?"

He sucked in a breath and glared at the ceiling. "Point made."

She laughed. "I'm delighted. It's about time you admitted this kind of thing isn't the norm of human behavior. Layla must be an amazing woman."

He stiffened. "What does she have to do with it?"

His sister laughed again. "Simple, Brett. She's the only thing that's changed in your life since the last time I talked to you."

LAYLA PUMPED HARDER at the pedal with her right foot, sending her potter's wheel spinning faster. She bent forward, concentrating intently on the shape she wanted, splaying her fingers, bringing them up, now tighter, now looser, molding, guiding, keeping the pressure steady, slackening, slackening, nearly there, nearly there...

Good.

Now the tricky part. She shot her arms out of the loose sleeves of her work smock, bent her elbows and approached carefully, slowly. Just to shape it a bit thinner, bring the open shape even more—

Damn.

The neck of the vase wobbled off to one side, then parted company with the rest of the clay form and splatted onto the side of the wheel, where it spun forlornly, threatening to fling itself off the edge unless she stopped pedaling.

She'd nearly gotten it. Close. A long, graceful sweep, rounded slightly, opening like a flower to a trumpet-shaped neck.

Okay, not that close.

She sighed, pounded the clay into a shapeless lump and scraped the whole mess off into her hands. Her time here had been half wasted. She was working on a piece for a client in California and had all the artistic inspiration of a cornflake. Nothing quite satisfied her, nothing jumped up and screamed perfection. The usual energy that flowed through her fingers, communicating ideas that shaped the clay, had been hijacked by a different kind of energy. In the end she couldn't tell if today's creations were really as awful as they seemed, or if she was simply not in the mood to judge.

She dumped the clay back into the bucket, covered it with plastic and thumped the lid into place, protecting the moisture inside. At least the time alone with her wheel in this rough shack she'd built herself, with the supple yielding clay under her hands, had steadied her mood and brought her some welcome perspective.

Brett Devlin could cause only as much trouble as she let him. He wasn't an inconsiderate guest, though *guest* was hardly an appropriate word. He'd tried small talk, then when she'd made it clear she didn't care for meaningless chatter, he'd stopped. He'd helped around the house, or tried to, clumsily, and she was apparently a territorial control freak, having lived alone for so long, able to do everything her own way.

When he'd stopped making lunch to stare at her, she'd suddenly heard herself issuing instructions as if making peanut-butter sandwiches was a highly technical and dangerous mission not to be taken lightly. She must have sounded like a nutcase. Who cared how the sandwich was made? When had she gotten so rigid, all the while thinking of herself as such a free spirit up here on her mountain?

She pulled on her coat, checked the door of the shack's tiny woodstove to make sure it was closed, and went outside into the still-blowing snow, inhaling a deep breath of the damp chill and lifting her face to the pelting crystals. Whatever Brett had to tell her could wait until he chose to tell it. She'd adopt a Zen-like attitude. Live in the moment, not try to control what she couldn't control.

Enjoying his company might be a little out of the question, but at least she could try to be more civil.

She smiled and stooped to wipe her hands clean on the still rapidly accumulating snow. Nothing like time alone to recenter herself. Brett's arrival had shaken her badly; his continued presence in the house had kept her off balance, without time to regroup and analyze. Time at her wheel did that for her. She felt a lot more like her old self—serene, in control, stable.

She straightened and began trudging back through the near foot of powdery white, annoyed at the fact that her serene, in-control, stable heart beat faster and faster the closer she came to her cabin and to Brett.

CHAPTER SIX

LAYLA WALKED INTO the cabin to find Brett moving around, showered and shaved, dark hair curling, still wet, over his forehead. Baby was cradled peacefully in his arm, looking absurdly tiny next to his broad chest.

"I helped myself to your shower." He looked at her as if he half expected her to fly into a rage at the idea. Had she been that bad?

"Fine." She stepped out of her boots and discovered that smiling at him in a friendly way wasn't as difficult as she must have thought it would be. "When did Baby wake up?"

He looked at her curiously. "About ten minutes ago."

"Was she upset?"

He shook his head. "At least not as upset as I was."

Layla raised her eyebrows.

He grinned disarmingly, making her attitude toward him soften further. "I'm not exactly an expert with infants."

Layla shrugged and unzipped her parka, shaking her hair to clear it of snow. "She doesn't seem to mind."

He looked down at the peaceful child. "No."

Layla hung up her parka and reached for Baby, feeling awkward at the transferral of the child to her own care, and overconscious of where her hands and arms made contact with Brett's. Baby abruptly ended her reign of peace and broke into squalls that could probably be heard down in Leavenworth.

"Nice lungs."

Layla rolled her eyes in mock annoyance and made a beeline for her rocking chair to nurse. A minute later she was shifting uneasily, as if in the past two months and who knew how many nursings, she hadn't figured out the exact position she needed to be comfortable.

He was watching her, she could tell. Not frequent glances, not casual interest, not a glazed thinking-about-something-else gaze, but an intense, appraising stare. It was driving her nuts, in spite of her determination to be Zenlike. Maybe if she turned to stare back, he'd get the message.

He didn't.

Instead he took it as some kind of permission to come closer, to stare more openly and take a seat way too near her once again, on the cedar chest.

"It's an amazing thing to be able to feed your child with your body."

She shrugged. "All mammals do. It's pretty basic machinery."

"I guess." Hands on his thighs, he leaned forward as he had that morning when he'd talked about intruding into her life. "My sister has a foster child the same age as yours. Also a little girl."

"Your sister Shana?"

"Yes."

"Who this morning you told me was part of your delirium last night? A product of lunatic ravings? *That* sister Shana?" She smiled sweetly. *Gotcha.*

His eyes narrowed, then a slow smile spread across his face with something that looked like admiration.

"Right." He leaned back and crossed his arms over his chest, always the cool customer. "That sister Shana."

"I see." Layla nodded ever-so-politely. Point scored, time to move on. If she'd learned nothing else, she'd learned that pushing this man got her nothing but back strain and skinned palms. "What happened to the baby's parents?"

He made an odd little shift with his eyes, as if he'd been caught talking about something he shouldn't be talking about. "She hopes to get the little girl back to her birth mother soon."

"Oh." Layla looked back down at Baby, feeling inadequate as usual in expressing whatever small-talk-type sentiments were called for. "That's nice."

A particularly strong gust of wind hit the cabin. Baby startled, arm flung out and rigid, then slowly let her tiny hand drift back down to the top of Layla's breast.

Layla gritted her teeth. There was more she should say to Brett about his sister and her foster child, more she felt, but getting emotions out in appropriate words wasn't a strength of hers.

"A child should be with its mother."

"Yes." He said the word as if it had tremendous significance, which made Layla even more bewildered and uncomfortable. She could survive alone on top of a mountain and take care of herself admirably, but when it came to making conversation, she was as inept as Baby. Unable to pick up the proper cues or say the right soothing things. Another reason she loved her life alone. That pressure wasn't on her except on her rare visits to Leavenworth.

He watched until Baby finished eating, then tactfully turned away when Layla released the suction and burped her. He seemed content with the silence, which put Layla a little more at ease. Maybe his chatter of the morning had been the exception, not the rule. Maybe he'd been trying to make her comfortable, though he'd accomplished quite the opposite.

She put Baby in her infant seat, strapped her black, white and red cow-shaped wrist rattle on, gave her head a kiss and walked over to the kitchen. Her instinct was to boil water for her usual comforting pasta dinner, but the sandwich thing still smarted.

She had a steak in the refrigerator, a rare treat she could indulge in only after her trips to Leavenworth, given the miniscule size of her gas refrigerator's freezer space. She also had greens for a salad and ice cream for dessert. Brett would reap the benefit of her trip to town, lucky him.

He'd gotten up from the chest and followed her. She didn't need to hear his lopsided footsteps to know, his presence was so strong behind her. But even as she braced for panic and claustrophobia, she realized panic and claustrophobia weren't coming. No threat, no feeling of being crowded. Her session at the wheel had really made a difference.

"Can I help with dinner?"

"Sure, thanks." She patted herself on the back for continuing to react calmly. This was a good chance to prove to him—and to herself—that she didn't have to add obsessive-compulsive to her other flaws. She got the salad greens out and a bowl, and pushed them toward him on the counter. "The lettuce is already washed. I do it when I get back from the store. It saves time in the long run."

"Right." He began tearing the lettuce into bite-size

pieces, but she had the distinct impression something she'd said had amused him.

Whatever. Layla Marino must be a regular comedy act to a whole lot of people. She put two cups of water on to boil and measured out a cup of rice.

He cleared his throat. "Can I suggest something?"

Her hand tightened around the measuring cup and she forced it to relax. "Sure."

"If you sauté the rice in butter or olive oil first, then add only one and a half times the water, with a bouillon cube, the rice comes out fluffier and more flavorful."

Her hand tightened again. She considered pouring the rice in the cup on his head, watching it trickle down through this thick hair to splash in a gentle flurry on her floor, a lovely reflection of the weather.

But she didn't.

"Sounds good. I'll try it." Her voice came out through clenched teeth and she forced a smile. Why was she being so resentful? Her rice was always a bland wet mess. Maybe he was right. Fluffy and more flavorful would be a nice change.

A minute later, the sautéing rice released a nutty fragrance into the air, and she was searching for bouillon cubes in her cupboard. That wasn't so hard. See? She could be flexible.

She added water and the cube, covered the pot and set the flame on low, her tension rising as she waited for further criticism. None came.

"Anything else for the salad?"

She frowned. "Anything else?"

He looked at her curiously. "Onion, tomato, cucumber, garlic, oregano."

She stared back at him, remembering her years waiting tables, remembering all the variations in salad composition and texture and seasonings she'd run across. Her first years here, she'd cooked grandly, experimented wildly. Then, long before Baby came along and made complicated meals impossible, she'd slowly cut back. To lettuce. With oil and vinegar and salt. Period.

Her stomach started churning; she felt a strange strangled sensation in her chest. When had she gotten into such a rut? And why? She didn't like the reflection of herself this man was showing her. She didn't want to see herself this way. She wanted to be alone, didn't want him here, didn't want *anyone*—

"Layla?" Brett spoke gently, kindly, as if he was soothing a small child in the middle of her worst nightmare.

"What? What is it?"

He reached out and patted her head, unbearably patronizing. "If the salad thing is too radical, I understand."

She stared at him in horrified disbelief, then caught the mischief in his eyes. Undignified and totally unexpected laughter burst out of her and made her glad she had nothing in her mouth, or he would have been thoroughly sprayed.

Though he kind of deserved it.

Brett raised his hands and shrugged helplessly. "I mean, after the Great Peanut-Butter Impasse..."

She meant to glare at him, but more laughter came instead, as if it had a mind of its own and didn't care at all about how she wanted to appear to him.

"I mean, you know, we can just leave it this way. Lettuce. In a bowl." He uttered the words as if all hope for the universe was lost, picked up a leaf, gazed at it mournfully, then let it plop back into the salad. "I'd really hate to rock your world."

Layla gasped and snorted. Then the laughter seemed to catch her weird fears about herself and her existence and all the tension concerning his stay here, and turn them into more laughter until she was all but doubled over, tears streaming, her stomach protesting to the point of pain. "Stop! *Stop!*"

She fought for control, heard him chuckling as her hysteria eased. Finally her stomach muscles loosened, laughter still bubbling up but only occasionally spilling out.

"Oh." She took a deep breath and held her hand to her chest, breathless, glowing, feeling changed somehow...lightened. "I haven't laughed that hard since I was a kid."

"Really?" He gave her a penetrating look that made some distinctly unfunny things happen to her insides. "What happened then?"

She blew out a sigh and dragged the heels of her hands over the wetness on her cheeks. "What do you mean?"

"What made you laugh this hard the last time?"

Her hands slowed and stopped on her jaw. She remembered. One of the migrant workers, a real bastard alcoholic waste of oxygen named Carlo, had come on to her a little too forcefully. She'd had to fend guys off once in a while, and most of them respected her. But he'd been lit by something that night, something that went deeper than alcohol-fueled lust. For the first time she had doubted her ability to turn a man away.

She could still remember the panic clawing at her. He was repulsive even from a distance, but close up...

Then, like a hero riding in on his stallion, her friend

Pedro had burst into the stuffy little room in the trailer, brandishing a thick shiny weapon and a fierce get-your-hands-off-her attitude that had made him seem years older than a teenager. She wasn't sure who had been more stunned—her or Carlo, who had muttered an apology and staggered out of the room, eyeing the weapon fearfully.

Not until he was gone did she get a close look at this terrifying club Pedro had brandished in the dim room.

A cucumber.

They'd practically wet themselves laughing, relief and shock over the passed danger, hilarity at the absurdity of the rescue. It had also been the first time she'd seen Pedro as anything but the giant gentle boy he'd always seemed. They'd become close friends and then each other's first lover.

She wasn't sure where he was. She hoped he was happy. Maybe she should look him up someday.

Layla brought her hands down from her face, where they'd been stuck while she'd taken her trip down memory lane. Brett must be wondering what the hell she was thinking. "An old friend, a childish prank. Funny at the time."

He nodded, but she got the feeling he'd seen more than that in her silent remembering. "Laughter is good for you. Releases tension, massages the heart, produces endorphins. You should do it more often."

She wiped her eyes, feeling awkward, as if he'd been watching her do something very private. Which in a way he had. She had the uneasy feeling that she could just as easily have been sobbing as laughing. Except she never cried.

"Well, thanks. Except life isn't that funny."

He started to answer. He got that probing intense look in his eyes again, and she wasn't in the mood for it.

"You can put whatever you want in the salad. I have some carrots in the vegetable bin and some onions in the cabinet there." She pointed to her modern version of a root cellar—a storage area covered by a bright red curtain in the far corner away from the fire. "I don't buy much perishable stuff for obvious reasons."

"Obvious?" He tipped his head in an inquisitive way, as if he guessed the answer but wanted her version.

"I only go to town once a month." She seasoned the steak with salt and pepper, then sent him a sly look. "Salt and pepper okay, or do you require white truffle oil?"

He grinned. "If it's good beef, you don't need more."

"I agree." She put her iron frying pan on the stove to heat, her heart curiously light, her body tired but strong and relaxed, as if she'd put in good hours of physical labor. She felt like humming while she worked, or bursting out into full song. She used to sing quite a bit as she worked around the cabin. Folk tunes mostly, or singers her parents loved. Joni Mitchell, Jackson Browne, Crosby, Stills, Nash and Young. Hadn't done that for a while, either.

"Why do you live up here by yourself?"

Layla's urge to warble vanished, though she stopped short of throwing him a mind-your-own business glance. She'd promised to wear her pleasant skin. And, to be honest, the last ten minutes or so had been more than pleasant, they'd been downright enjoyable. Giddy even. The laughing fit had released a lot of her tension. She didn't want to ruin their truce entirely. And, truthfully, that was exactly the question she'd ask if their positions were reversed. She didn't have to answer with her life story.

"I like being alone." She reached into the cupboard and glimpsed the bottles of wine she kept for times when she felt like celebrating. This wasn't particularly a time for celebration, but wine would be good with steak, and Brett might appreciate it.

"That's it? You just like it?"

She held up the bottle and two glasses in a silent question and he nodded.

"You're not running from the law? Or scarred by some childhood trauma?"

Even at his half-teasing tone, she felt her expression change. By the sharpened interest in his face, she was sure he'd noticed before she could school her features. She wasn't used to having to hide anything. Wasn't used to the games people had to play to be around each other. Her entire childhood had been a trauma. Not that there hadn't been fun and friendship along the way. But the scars ran deeper than the healing times could erase.

She poured him a glass of wine and a quarter-glass for herself.

He raised an eyebrow. "Not much of a drinker?"

"I don't want Baby to get too much."

He gave her that curious look again and she realized she'd forgotten to use Baby's real name. "Phoebe shouldn't have too much alcohol."

The name felt clumsy on her tongue and made the whole situation worse. She picked up her glass and took a healthy sip, then turned her back on him to cook the steak, responding to his offer of more help by assigning him to set the table.

They finished preparing dinner in a less-than-comfortable silence, which lasted until they both sat to eat. Baby, in typical fashion, chose that moment as her time of greatest need.

Layla sighed wearily. The thing she missed most about her pre-mom life was undisturbed meals.

"You eat." Brett gestured to her plate and picked Baby up before she could move. "I'm sure you get a lot of this."

She stifled both her surprise and her instinctive objection to his generosity. Why shouldn't she take advantage of baby-sitting for the few days he was here? And Baby's fuss saved her from another intimate tête-à-tête meal.

She ate, watching as he cradled the child, hobbling around the room, occasionally saying something in a low, soothing voice she could barely hear. The meal was delicious. And eating it without a child in her lap or attached to her breast was delicious, too. She was admittedly grateful to Brett.

Except...she was enjoying it too much. Sitting here, having something simple being done for her. Watching a man enjoy himself with her child. It was pleasurable. It was thoughtful of him.

It was making her very uneasy.

Because her next thought was going to be how nice it would be to have someone to help her out more often. And she couldn't let her mind go in that direction. She needed to eat and to enjoy this unexpected moment of peace for what it was. An isolated incident in a life that would go forward as she planned, alone.

Her last bite swallowed, she jumped to take Baby

while Brett ate, then washed the dishes, uneasy again when he automatically stepped in to help dry. Uneasy that she appreciated his contribution to her work routine. As soon as she could, she'd escape this companionable functioning and feed Baby, who was settled happily in her seat. Layla didn't want to get used to any part of this.

She let Baby nurse longer than usual, urging the child to fight off sleep and accept more food, her once-again-jangled nerves welcoming the private familiar moment with her child. If only she could block out the male presence in the room more effectively. She knew where he was every second, how he was sitting on the couch, resting his ankle on her old trunk *cum* coffee table. She knew what his eyes looked like gazing into the fire, how his brow furrowed into brooding when he thought no one was watching. Even if she wasn't looking directly at him, she knew.

This man had something heavy on his mind, maybe something heavy on his soul. She wished she didn't want to know what it was. She hoped it had nothing to do with what he had to tell her.

Finally and inevitably, Baby lost the battle against sleep. Layla put the little one in her crib, smoothed her hair, and realized now she had no choice but to start an intimate evening with Brett.

For the first time ever, she wished she had a TV.

She scowled and brought herself back to reality. The man was probably still exhausted from his injuries, as anxious as she was to end the evening. He'd probably jump at the chance to read one of her library books, even if science fiction wasn't his thing.

She turned to find Brett with newly refilled wineglasses, his full, hers again at one-quarter. He was sitting on the floor in front of the fire, his injured ankle propped up on a cushion, his walking stick leaning against her sofa, which, now that she looked, bore the marks of spills and burns from the previous owner, and grime from years of woodstove fires. He held her glass up to her and indicated she should join him, fire lighting his features in a shadowy, mysterious way that made him startlingly attractive.

So much for library books.

Layla stood, torn between the idea of sitting in front of the fire, sipping more wine—she'd been so careful, a little more wouldn't hurt—and reading her book by herself. Baby had come into her life as a result of a glass of wine, a fire and an attractive stranger. She didn't want to make the same mistake twice.

She gave a wry smile and moved slowly forward. *Pinch yourself, you're dreaming.* Layla Marino was older and a damn sight wiser now. This man was not the sweet serious Rick who'd lost his way and arrived at her cabin by some miracle, dehydrated and disoriented. This man had a definite motive for being here, which stood between them as effectively as a chastity belt.

She sat with a good three feet of worn burgundy Oriental rug between them and accepted the wine. The fire wavered and danced in the stove, logs glowing orange at the base of the yellow flame.

"Baby's asleep?"

She nodded curtly, unsure if he'd picked up on her nickname for the child or was simply referring to her impersonally. Taking a guilty sip of wine, she let it smooth over her tongue.

"Where is her father?"

The wine shot down her throat in a convulsive swallow. Where had *that* come from? Did his wanting to know shoot her theory of Rick sending Brett to find her?

"No question too personal?"

He turned from contemplating the fire and contemplated her in a serious thoughtful way that made his eyes look even deeper brown than they already were. She felt the shock of attraction again, more powerfully than before, a shock that jolted immediately down to where it was most dangerous. *Trouble. Trouble again.* She gazed into her glass, swirling the liquid while she struggled to control the growing longing in her body.

"You interest me. You intrigue me, actually. Why a beautiful young woman would want to hide herself away like this..."

Layla shut out the seductive tone and gripped her annoyance as if it were a life raft. "I'm not hiding. I live here because I like to be alone. That's it."

"Sure. Okay." He held her gaze, calm and unapologetic, and might as well have said, *You are such a liar.*

She drank more wine, anger churning her stomach. "It's my business what I do with my life."

"Did I imply otherwise?"

She really—*really*—wanted to hurl the rest of her wine in his smug face, but she took another sip instead. "No. But you keep asking me."

"Because I want to know."

"I've *told* you."

He smiled, an infuriating know-it-all smile. "At the risk of making this worse—no. You haven't. Not really."

Her temper flared, pushing her up on her knees, until his hand stopped her, clamping down firmly on her arm. She tried to wrest it away, but he held her. "Don't get angry. Stay."

The gentle words stopped her. If he'd tried to apologize or rationalize, he only would have angered her more.

She let herself back down grudgingly, spine still rigid, not sure why she let herself be manipulated into anger or its deflation. "You know nothing about me."

"And you'd like to keep it that way." He was looking at her again, in that way that was so thorough, so compelling that half of her wanted to run away screaming and the other half wanted to stay and immerse herself in it.

"Yes. I have no idea who you are. I'm not interested in spilling my life story to a stranger."

"Fair enough." He took a sip of wine, then another. She had the impression his calm was giving way to unsettled energy, and it unnerved her.

"How about if I tell you about me? Then I won't be a stranger."

"*What?*" Her heart gave a jump of excitement, then just as quickly turned wary.

"My story. 'About Me,' by Brett Devlin." He took another sip of wine and placed his arm on his raised knee, the rest of his body stretched and lean, firelight glinting on the ruby wine. He looked like the cover model on a damn men's magazine.

"Let's see. I was born in Detail, Nebraska, in 1970. My dad was a hardworking middle-class guy, an accountant. My mother was a housewife with too much time on her hands and too much anger in her brain." His smooth tone roughened, his body grew less relaxed.

"Brett…" Layla didn't want to hear about him,

didn't want him to be real in any way, wanted him to stay nothing but a vaguely threatening attractive stranger she could comfortably push out of her mind. He was male and strong, lit by firelight, and she had wine in her veins and had been alone for a long, long time. "I don't think I want to hear this."

He turned toward her, eyes intent and sharply focused. "Why not?"

"Because…" She gestured in frustration. What the hell was she supposed to say? *Because if you become a real human being with a past and emotions and depth, I'll want to sleep with you even more than I do now.* "Never mind."

Baby stirred, whimpered, and settled. Layla blew out a relieved breath and tried to moisten her throat with another sip of wine, ending up with her throat feeling drier than ever. Beside her, Brett sat still, making her own nervous movements more obvious. At best, he thought her incredibly rude, cutting him off like that after he'd tried, for whatever reason, to share himself with her. At worst, he suspected the truth. Either way, although she'd been hoping for silence, she couldn't take this uncomfortable one anymore.

"I'm sorry. I'm not used to…people anymore." She bit the sentence off. For God's sake, she sounded like some being from another planet. *I am not used to the ways of you humans.* She couldn't be *that* bad. "What I mean is…"

"It's okay." He sat back, staring at the fire. She saw pain in his eyes and a hint of vulnerability, and in one startlingly intuitive moment, realized he'd actually wanted to unburden himself to her. Maybe he didn't realize it even now, or maybe he did and it was a surprise.

Regardless, she'd stomped all over his offering as though it were a creepy bug.

"Go ahead, Brett. I'm sorry."

He turned those keen eyes on her again. "Why the change?"

She swallowed, held his gaze. "I just freaked a little. I haven't heard many life stories lately."

"I can imagine. Unless you have magic-talking squirrels in the forest."

"No." She smiled and shook her head. "No magic squirrels. Just me and Baby, and she isn't saying much yet, in words anyway."

"That'll change."

"Yes." She hunched her shoulders and stared at her glass of wine. "I...want to hear. About you."

She did, God help her. She'd ruined the moment out of her own fear and panic, and not until this minute did she realize how much she wanted it back.

"Okay."

She peeked at him after several seconds had passed and saw him staring at the fire. Was he not sure how to get back into the story? Had he changed his mind about sharing himself?

She swallowed and fingered her glass. "How did your...dad deal with your mother?"

For another minute he stared at the fire. Layla's heart sank. The moment had passed. He wasn't going to answer.

"My dad developed an attraction for a co-worker. I don't know what, if anything, happened, or how my mom found out. Dad swore nothing did happen, to us and to her. And he was the kind of guy who always admitted his mistakes. Always taught us to admit to ours."

His voice slowed, as if the words were having trouble coming out of his mouth, as if he was slowly losing power to transmit them. "He was thrown out of the house on twenty-four hours' notice, no second chance, not allowed to come near us again at home, though he'd contact us at school sometimes and take us out to lunch."

Layla put her wine down, as if she was getting rid of a glass of poison. She'd asked for it and she was getting it. Her heart already ached with sympathy. She knew what it felt like as a child to wish every day with your entire body that your life was anything but what it was.

"He never married again, never got over my mother for whatever masochistic reason. When he'd show up to see us, I used to be furious at how sad and lost he looked. I'd want to scream at him to have some pride."

His words came out low and furious, his eyes glazed and fierce, reflecting the heat of the fire. "I swore I'd never let anyone control me to that degree. I hated him for his weakness. My mom remarried a decent guy, but by then I was too angry to care and I sure as hell didn't want to stick around and watch that marriage turn sour."

"God, Brett." Her voice came out desperate and frightened; she picked up her wine again and clutched it to her chest as if the cool glass could offer her comfort.

This was worse than she thought. She didn't want to feel all this, didn't want to feel the deep connection of understanding—an alienated, lonely youth that led to building protective walls in adulthood. His in whatever isolation he chose; hers in this cabin.

A log rolled off the burning pile in the woodstove. Layla jumped to prod it back into place and add another before she sat back down, a little farther away this time.

The action broke some of the power of the spell woven by his words. Now maybe they could be nearly strangers again, having a friendly-as-possible-given-the-circumstances glass of wine in front of the fire.

Except the images wouldn't leave her alone. He had a sister, he said, who took in foster children. An attempt to give love to children since she hadn't had enough herself growing up? How many people spent their entire adulthoods compensating for unhappy childhoods? What a waste it seemed, and how incomprehensible it must be to those she'd envied all her life, the kids who'd grown up in healthy, loving suburban stability.

How had Brett reacted? How had he structured his life?

"What do you do now?"

"I'm a private investigator." He lifted his glass in a toast to her. "I specialize in finding missing people."

She swallowed, her curiosity about social theory dwindling into the reality of their situation. "I'm not missing."

He grinned and reached to touch the side of her face, another brief touch, which left her wanting it to have lasted longer. "Not anymore."

"Someone hired you to find me."

"Yes." He took another sip of his wine, then drained the glass in one gulp, as if the tiny tastes had gotten irritating and unfulfilling. "I told you that."

She bit the inside of her cheek. Regardless of his

childhood, he was a stubborn son-of-a-b right now. The intimate, cozy, drinks-by-the-fire atmosphere vanished under her irritation. She got to her feet.

Brett followed the movement with his head. "Going to bed?"

"Yes."

He narrowed his eyes at the abrupt syllable, taking in her mood as usual. "I guess I'll turn in, too."

He brought his ankle up off the pillow, wincing slightly, and twisted onto his knees to stand. Layla instinctively moved forward to offer her arm, which he took, then laid a hand on her shoulder to climb to his feet. To her surprise, he left the hand there, grasped her other shoulder, and held her much too close to him.

She forced herself not to pull back, her initial instinctive claustrophobia giving way to the wonderful sensation of the warmth and strength in his hands. Her weakness for touch had gotten her in trouble before. When would she learn?

He opened his mouth to speak. She could see a battle raging inside him. Was he wondering what to say? Whether to say it? How to say it?

Obviously he hadn't made up his mind exactly how to handle her or the situation they'd been thrust in. She managed to hold his gaze calmly, noticing the faint shadows at the corners of his eyes, the curling dark lashes, the squarish, faintly stubbled line of his jaw.

Then her gaze caught foolishly, for one microsecond too long, on the clean lines of his mouth.

In that one microsecond the air changed. She'd been noticing his mouth, and he was standing too close to her, noticing that she'd noticed.

She swallowed, and the swallow made a harsh squeak in the silence.

"Good night," she whispered.

She had to pull away, had to get out of this crazy chemical moment and get back to reality.

His hands tightened on her shoulders; he sensed her desire to run. "It will be okay, Layla. It will all be okay."

She felt her calm gaze evaporate, felt the anxiety take over, and worse, the comforting protection of his arms going around her in a brief hug that she wanted to last all night.

"Good night." He moved away, leaving her shocked and suddenly chilly. He bent for his walking stick, took two steps toward her bed, then stopped.

"Layla."

"Yes." She dropped her head and turned it slightly away so he couldn't tell she'd been watching him.

"You sleep in your own bed tonight."

She started to shake her head, but he held up a hand. "No argument. I've been enough of a bother to you."

She wanted to argue, but arguing meant more talking, more looking at him, so damn magnificent in the firelight. Right now she wanted to be horizontal with her eyes tightly shut, preferably unconscious in sleep, to escape him and the memory of those brief moments of human contact.

God, what a weakness. She and Rick had been friendly, with none of this crackling hostility, crackling truce. Their lovemaking had come gently, evolved naturally out of mutual need. Lovemaking with this man would be—

Stop. She put the emergency brakes on her thoughts. Lovemaking was not at issue here. Even with the risk of pregnancy pretty much out of the picture for a full-time nursing mom, she needed to remember that after Rick had left, she'd been plunged for weeks into a depression which had little to do with hormones. She needed to remember that the freer she kept herself from human entanglements, the happier she was.

But most of all she needed to forget what Brett Devlin looked like when he wanted to kiss a woman.

CHAPTER SEVEN

BRUCE LEHR DROVE UP to their house in Madison Park, a spacious white Colonial overlooking Lake Washington. Anne was out front, wearing one of his old overcoats, putting the finishing touches on a whimsical papier-mâché creation with their neighbor's daughter, Bethany.

He pulled into the garage and came back out, grinning. Anne was made for motherhood. Endless patience, and energy, spirit and creativity to match... Had he mentioned he loved his wife?

Their wedding had been perfect. Quiet, small, just her family and their close friends, dinner after the ceremony and lots of champagne. They were postponing their honeymoon until the situation surrounding their hoped-for adoption of Jim's daughter was worked out. Anne had been willing to go, but he knew he'd spend the entire time checking messages. He owed her the honeymoon of her dreams and he'd deliver, even if they had to wait until the little girl went off to college.

He moved closer to the laughing pair and realized his first impression was wrong. Not just any papier-mâché creation. A turkey, life-size, complete with magnificent plumage, though he'd guess the green and pink feathers had been painted by Anne's five-year-old helper.

"Thanksgiving dinner?"

"Absolutely." She turned, rosy-cheeked and breathless from laughing, and kissed him warmly in spite of her cold lips. "Mmm. Hello. I missed you. How was your day?"

"Better now that I'm here." He smiled down at her, wondering how he'd survived the first thirty-two years of his life without her. "How was yours?"

"Some good, some bad. Getting a home business off the ground is agony. Bethany's mom had to run some errands so I said I'd watch her. I was glad for a break." She turned to include the little girl in their conversation. "We've been having so much fun, haven't we, Bethany?"

The blond five-year-old nodded, curls bouncing around her bright blue hat. "Yeah. We're a *team*. And this is Hilda."

"The turkey that will survive for many Thanksgivings to come." Anne winked.

Bruce laughed and hugged her to him, desperate to tell her the latest about Jim's daughter. "Well, team, how about we go inside for some hot chocolate and cookies, because I have some news."

Anne turned searching eyes to his. "Alycia?"

He nodded. "They found Layla. Near Leavenworth. The baby is doing well."

"Oh, gosh." Her eyes filled with tears. "Will she…will Layla agree to…give her up?"

"Who's Layla? Was she lost?" Bethany looked anxiously at Anne's face.

"Just for a little while, honey." Anne smiled gently at the girl. "But she's found now."

"That made you sad."

"Only for a second." Anne laid a playful hand on

Bethany's head. "Cocoa and cookies and we'll tell you a story."

Bruce offered one hand to Anne and the other to Bethany. "About a little baby girl who went on a big adventure on top of a mountain."

"Wow." Bethany fell into step beside him. "That sounds cool. Does she get to come home at the end?"

Anne could only manage a choked sound in reply. Bruce squeezed the little chilly hand in his, heart heavy with uncertainty. "Of course she does, sweetheart. Of course."

LITTLE ALYCIA LET OUT a cute chirpy sound, then went quiet. Brett couldn't say he knew a lot about babies, but this one sure slept a lot. He peeked cautiously into her crib to make sure she hadn't stopped breathing, or something equally terrifying. The wispy blond hair and that tiny, pouty mouth did something warm and fuzzy to his insides—and he didn't do warm and fuzzy.

Generally he regarded babies as evils necessary for the continuation of the species. Maybe his tender feelings were brought on by the uncertain future the little girl had. The snow had been slowing gradually all day; the radio predicted an end to it during the night. Which meant snowplows a day or two after that and a tow truck. He could be on his way, and Alycia's new life would begin.

Something twisted inside him at the thought of leaving. Not that he'd miss Layla, but he had grown strangely protective of her in the past couple of days, and the idea of leaving her alone to face his bad news was becoming less and less appealing. As much as he wanted to stick by his decision not to become emotionally involved in his cases, there was no question the current circumstances threatened to change that policy—maybe they already had.

Last night he told Layla things he'd told no one else. What started as a ploy to gain her trust, to make dumping the news a little easier on her, had backfired, grown and expanded into a *need* to tell this strange, fiery, independent woman where he'd come from, what he'd been through.

Worse, it had felt good—cleansing, like those incredibly annoying therapy-obsessed people insisted it would. It was as if some of his anger had leaked out with the words and left him calmer.

Calmer, that is, until he'd been holding Layla's shoulders to comfort her and caught those vulnerable hazel eyes looking at his mouth as if she wanted to devour it. He'd been instantly sideswiped by an intense, barely controllable urge to do the same to her.

He wasn't sure he could even begin to count the reasons that was a bad idea. Even thinking about it was a bad idea.

He focused his attention back on the crib. Baby Alycia scrunched her little face up in an expression of pain—or anger or pique—and relaxed it again into sleep, much to his relief. Who knew how much longer Layla would be out there with her potter's wheel? He'd just as soon the baby slept the whole time.

He moved steadily toward the kitchen area for a glass of water. His ankle was healing nicely, if slowly. The back of his head was still sensitive to the touch, but he didn't feel so fuzzy anymore. The Devlin brain was able to process thoughts in its usual sharp fashion. Lucky, since he had a lot of thoughts to process.

The icy liquid poured a chill down his throat,

through his chest and into his stomach. Layla was different with her child, more detached and matter-of-fact than the other mothers he'd seen, who talked constantly about their offspring and their amazing accomplishments, even if what ranked as amazing to them generally didn't make his list. Such as how many times the child had filled his or her diaper on any given night.

Even his own mother, who wouldn't win any awards for warmth or capacity for human intimacy, had constantly bored strangers with his and Shana's escapades, though always in a way that revolved around herself.

Layla's child seemed to occupy a practical, natural place in her life. She related to her the way he imagined pioneer women did to their children. Having to devote so much time to the chores involved in survival, they couldn't afford the luxury of doting.

Still, it seemed strange to him, and like a true P.I., he wanted to solve the mysteries inherent in Layla Marino. Why didn't she use the child's name? Why did she box herself away from humanity? Was she incapable of love or deep warmth? Didn't she need or crave human intimacy the way most people did? He was a loner himself, but he wouldn't be able to stand isolation to this degree.

Yet the chemistry between them last night had been unmistakable, and she hadn't shied entirely away from that. If anything she'd instigated it. And she'd conceived the child, so being intimate with another human being couldn't be that abhorrent.

How had her baby come to be? Had Layla wanted a child, gotten herself pregnant and sent the father on his way? Or had the jerk come along for a joyride and left her pregnant without a backward glance?

Had she loved him?

His glass thudded down onto her wooden counter, covered with red-and-white-checkered oilcloth. If the guy had hurt her, Brett would cheerfully track him down and break his neck.

He dragged his hand over his face and rubbed his chin. He didn't want to think about Layla with Phoebe's father, and he sure as hell didn't want to feel jealous anger at the thought of Layla loving the man. Brett had been with plenty of women, loved a few in a pleasant, friendly way, but jealousy had never been part of his makeup. Guys who felt jealous anger were in serious trouble. He'd never let himself get that far gone.

And despite the invitation in her eyes last night, he definitely wasn't about to let himself fall for a woman who wore a six-foot sign that read Private Property, Trespassers Will Be Shot On Sight. Not exactly relationship material.

He moved around the cabin, indulging a sudden restlessness, examining paintings on the walls, giving his ankle a light exercising to make it stronger. There were prints and paintings of wildlife and detailed landscapes. He liked and shared her taste for natural colors, understated views, for finding the remarkable in a close-up of the ordinary.

Admittedly, what made Layla tick, what had gone on in her past to make her live this way, still fascinated him. And the combination of his detective curiosity and, okay, personal interest, had fed that fascination into an obsession.

He limped past her pantry area, past the rows of

iron hooks on which hung keys, rain gear, mom and baby hats and parkas to a picture he'd overlooked before. A worn black-and-white photo of what appeared to be a group of migrant workers standing somberly in a field. Only one had smiled for the camera; the rest stood stiffly, looking like the old sepia portraits of Civil War regiments.

He focused on the smiling man, taller than the rest, not so dark. There was something odd about that smile, as if it was induced by an artificial substance, not the desire to communicate friendly feelings toward the camera. His hair was long, matted, pulled back in a sloppy ponytail. Brett had an eerie flash of intuition that he knew him, but the feeling passed before he could grab and examine it. Beside the man stood an old-before-her-time, equally bedraggled woman, also remarkable in the picture for being tall and fair.

Interesting. The portrait captured much of what he knew about the lives of migrant workers, which admittedly was not a lot. Fields in the background, a rattletrap truck, stacks of crates—were those strawberry plants? The out-of-place couple must have been what had caught Layla's artist eye to the photograph. He stared at it for another moment until the sound he'd been dreading exploded into the cabin.

Man, could that kid scream. And she hadn't woken up with a nice whimper, either. She'd gone zero to sixty in a split second.

He hobbled over and picked her up awkwardly, though her little body was so stiff from screaming that she came up in one tight little package, not flopping all over, body parts dangling.

He tucked the baby in the crook of his arm as he'd done before and rocked her gently.

No change in volume.

He switched her to his shoulder and patted her back as he'd seen Layla do.

Nothing doing.

He contemplated going out to the work shed and throwing himself on Layla's mercy, and just as quickly tossed the idea out. She must have free time in pitifully short supply these days. She'd told him the baby wouldn't need feeding for another hour. He could deal with this.

Right?

First attempt—the Grand Baby Tour, pointing out fascinating objects in the cabin and patiently, he thought, explaining their various uses. *This is the fireplace. No touch. Ouchie.*

All of which outraged her even more. He couldn't blame her; it was pretty annoying even to him.

In desperation, it occurred to him that fussy babies liked to be sung to.

Roughly thirty seconds later, he'd exhausted every lullaby he could think of, namely "Rock-a-Bye, Baby."

No luck.

Maybe she liked a more contemporary sound? He tried out an Ella Fitzgerald number, "I've Got The World On a String," which got him an approximately twenty-second respite before the baby volume kicked back up to what must be the top of the range.

He sighed, feeling more vulnerable and helpless than he had in his life, even more than when he'd had to pee in a bucket or fainted on top of Layla. And about as frustrated.

Maybe this baby liked to rock 'n' roll.

He cleared his throat and took a deep breath so he could compete with her in the decibel department.

"'I can't get no-o sa-tis-fac-shun. I can't get no-o sa-tis-fac-shun. And I try. And I try. And I try. And I try...'"

The baby quieted. He could hardly believe it. She actually liked his mangled version of the Rolling Stones hit. He felt jubilant, victorious, triumphant. He puffed out his chest, held the baby up and began a little man-baby boogie number, as best he could with his injured ankle, continuing the song at the top of his lungs. "'I can't *get* no...no-no-no, I can't *get* no...no-no—'"

A sound behind him made him turn around and freeze in horror.

Layla. Leaning against the door she must have come through—please God, only a second ago, laughing helplessly, almost as hard as she had when he'd teased her about her salad. He loved the way she looked when she laughed, the way she changed, lit up, cut loose and gave in to it, as if her real self were being allowed to crack through some cement coating.

He grinned sheepishly and shrugged, still holding the baby, which made the little body bob up and down. "Did you know she likes the Stones?"

Layla shook her head and laughed the last bit of her laughter. "That was a picture I'll never forget."

Their gazes stuck, as they had last night in front of the fire. His grin faded at the same time hers did. The idea of a memory of him being planted with her forever had broken his giddy mood, made him feel serious and strange, almost...wistful.

This could not be happening. Not to him. Not now. Not with her.

She walked toward him and took the baby; he resisted letting go. For a strange second as they stood there, both holding a child that had no blood connection to either of them, he had a terrifying and wonderful feeling of what it might be like to be part of a family of his own.

LAYLA SAT ON THE FLOOR in front of the fire, holding on to her glass of barely sipped Beaujolais.

Steak leftovers for dinner. Wine. Nursing Baby, then sitting here in front of the woodstove together. Total déjà vu.

Except the silence was tense, expectant, far from the companionable feel of last night when they'd first sat together. Was that coming from her? Or him? Or did they both have some secret agenda or thought that was making the air around them alive with possibilities. Was it that the snow had stopped and they both knew plows would come soon and Brett would leave? Or was it something more immediate and...personal?

She scooted forward to put the wine on her trunk-slash-coffee table. Alcohol was the last thing she needed right now, mucking up her judgment. The man next to her was doing a damn good job of that all on his own.

The moment she'd walked in from her potting shed, where her creativity had once again been hijacked by thoughts of him, and found him bellowing out a half-decent version of the Stones to her enthralled child, something turned the rest of the way over in her heart and she hadn't managed to recover perspective or equilibrium.

Worse, she wasn't sure she cared.

How incredible that someone like Brett and someone like Rick had found her here in the middle of nowhere. It wasn't as if she would be attracted to any guy who wandered by—the creep she'd given the souvenir memory of a shotgun shell whizzing by his ear on his way out certainly knew that. Living alone hadn't made her desperate. But the two of them had arrived like signs from God that it was okay to feel passion once in a while. Maybe to indulge it.

She still didn't know what had brought Brett here, or what kind of news he was planning to spring on her. But that wouldn't change, whether or not she indulged herself in the meantime. Maybe she wasn't meant to live among people, but she wasn't a nun. And a private investigator from Nebraska wasn't going to interfere with her life after he left, beyond whatever reason he'd wanted to find her.

It all sounded perfectly sane. Except some deep instinct told her that this man would be more dangerous to her peace of mind than Rick had been. Not that she could possibly have developed any depth of feeling for him in two days. But Brett had turned out to be unexpectedly easy to have around.

Rick had fit in by being virtually invisible. He'd constantly wandered off by himself to explore or to meditate, which suited her fine. Obviously, Brett wasn't in any shape to go wandering off, especially during a blizzard, but his presence here, while galling at first, had evolved in such a short time to where he felt more like a partner in the house than an intruder.

Once he'd seen her routines, he'd mastered them, teasing her gently about some of her more rigid habits, making her laugh and lighten up. He'd quietly fixed a few things she'd gotten used to living with or just hadn't gotten around to mending since Baby had come into her life—the wobbly chair at the kitchen table, the peeling section of oilcloth on her counter.

Little moments, such as when she'd been laughing so hard over his singing, or when they'd both had their hands on Baby at the same time. Little moments that felt like he—

She amputated the thought. Belonged here? Was she *nuts?* He didn't belong here in the slightest. At most, she was realizing that for all her staunch soapbox denial, her life was indeed lonely at times.

Well, tough.

She'd chosen that loneliness one particular week her senior year in high school. Her parents had shown up to her school play, wasted and dirty, and passed out in the audience—unusual even for them—causing an uproar that interrupted the performance and made her the target of furious wannabe actors for days afterward, as if the usual torture wasn't enough.

The next day she'd come home from school, having been the butt of jokes and jeering all day, to find her parents sprawled dead on the floor, apparent victims of their own greed, caught trying to double cross the organization they ran drugs for. The verdict was "accidental overdose." The police weren't interested in investigating a double homicide in this case. Who cared? It wasn't as if her parents were real people.

So much for parental pride. So much for peer support. So much for the authorities. So much for humankind in general. After a lifetime of crowds and derision and prejudice and near-slavery, she'd decided right then that she'd find some way to live away from it all.

Not as easy as it had sounded.

She'd wanted a simple existence, but comfortable,

not more miserable poverty, and that meant money. Without the continuing support and encouragement of Karen Packard at Sunshine Kids, a program for gifted migrant worker children, she'd never have made it. For the next three exhausting years, she'd waited tables and cleaned houses and taken pottery classes until she turned twenty-one and unexpectedly inherited the property from grandparents who'd disowned her mother years before.

Miraculously, all her dreams had come true at once.

If she lived to be a thousand, she'd never, ever forget the exhilaration of freedom, of safety, of coming home that she'd experienced coming up this mountain the first time to her very own private version of heaven.

"I was looking at your pictures earlier today."

"Oh?" She brought herself severely back to reality and glanced around the cabin walls at her artworks. The landscape by Sika Dreehan from Oregon, who'd bought one of her serving platters and struck up a correspondence friendship. The pencil detail of a pinecone with needles that Karen Packard had given her years ago. Other prints she'd bought on trips to town... Her eyes flicked to the picture of her parents, then away.

Someday she might find peace with the way they'd lived and the way they'd died, but she hadn't managed to yet. The picture was a sometimes torturous reminder of who she was and why she lived here. Which was, somewhat perversely, why she'd put it on her wall in the first place, though she rarely looked at it.

"I see." She wasn't sure what else to say, but he'd started looking at her curiously and she had to say something.

"We share the same taste." He was still looking at her speculatively. Then he glanced at the picture of her parents and back. "What about that one?"

Layla hunched her shoulders. Like the arrow that found Achilles' one vulnerable spot. He probably noticed her face change when she registered the photograph. Mr. Private Investigator missed nothing. Being around someone so in tune with her emotions was invasive, irritating and…strangely thrilling.

She made herself relax. "It's a picture."

Dark brows lowered slightly over those invade-your-mind eyes, making him look concerned and thoughtful. "Want to tell me about it?"

His voice was quiet and gentle, the kind of voice that says, "It's safe to confide in me."

To her horror, a painful lump settled into her throat. He sat there, silent and patient, next to her, as if he'd be happy waiting even if it took her all night to get up the courage.

Her shoulders crept back up; she wrapped her arms around her knees. Did she want to tell him? She'd told Rick about her past in a dry recitation of facts while they'd been picnicking on a hike. Obviously the events of her life were a far cry from his Norman Rockwell upbringing, but he'd nodded thoughtfully, pushed his wire-rimmed glasses up his nose and squeezed her knee in a comforting way that had charmed her, warmed her, made her glad for the moment of human connection to savor after he left.

She did want to tell Brett. The certainty came with an unexpected rush. She wanted to tell him, to unburden herself and to feel that connection again.

But the words jammed up against the lump of fear and misery in her throat, and nothing would come out.

Damn. *Damn.* Why couldn't she do this? Why was it so much harder with this man than it had been with Rick?

Brett put his wine down on the table, and before his next move even registered, shocked the hell out of her by putting his arms around her—a knee-hugging, balled-up creature way too close to tears.

She tensed against the need to lean into him, one…two…three seconds, then his warmth and his strength and the fabulous male smell of him were too much and she gave in, fit her head under his jaw, let her body curl against his broad chest and felt her pain and tension start to ease away into pleasure and peace.

"My parents."

He moved his head against her hair. "Yes?"

"The people in the picture." Blissfully she closed her eyes and instructed her senses to memorize every possible nuance of what it felt like to be in his arms, to remember when she was alone again. "The tall ones. They're my parents."

Surprise tensed his body, then she felt him relax deliberately. "I thought the smile on the man was familiar."

She lifted her head and stared in mock horror. "I smiled at you? What a slip!"

He grinned, and the sight of that grin so close and so warm just about undid her. She lowered her head again, so her forehead touched his collarbone, and watched a tiny spider traverse the vast landscape of her rug toward his jeans-clad hips.

"You grew up with migrant workers."

"Yes."

"Tough life." The usual horror and disdain were missing from his voice. Instead she heard quiet sympathy, respect, maybe even admiration. "Lot of moving around. Lot of people around all the time."

She nodded and her forehead rubbed against the thick, soft material of his shirt.

"Maybe some people didn't always treat you with respect."

"Yes."

"Maybe some people made you feel like the dirt they thought you were."

"Maybe." She couldn't do more than whisper the word into the space so close to his body.

"That's why you live alone."

"Yes." She turned her face to the side, wanting to steal a little more contact with his warmth.

The movement brought her face back into the curve of his neck and set something in motion. Something in the air, something between them. She felt his body change from a comforting friendly presence to a purely male one. Her heart started thumping; she held still, waiting, her cheek against his shirt.

"Layla." He pulled his hand up her back in a warm sweep, let it settle briefly at the back of her neck, then explored her hair, filtering it through his fingers.

She closed her eyes, swallowed and tipped her face up, closer to that stretch of him not covered with clothing, between his collar and jaw. She stopped there, breath quick and high, little puffs that bounced against his skin.

His arms went stiff, his hand stopped moving through her hair.

She stretched forward in underwater slow motion, drawn by a need she barely understood, as well as the one she understood all too well, and touched her lips to that warm male skin. She let them rest there, inhaling his scent in a slow deep breath of pleasure.

His large hands tightened, cupping her head hard through her hair. He brought her face up toward his, his features blank.

"What are you doing?"

"I don't know." She whispered the words, bewildered, every muscle tense, back on guard.

"You don't *know?*"

"I think I'm out of my mind."

"Well, you're sure as hell driving me out of mine."

She waited, breathless, studying his face, totally unable to read his mood. "Is that good or bad?"

"It's bad, Layla."

Oh, no. Mortification flooded her. She moved her head to release it from his tight grip, but he brought her face toward him again. She could see anger and frustration in the features he'd controlled so well only seconds before.

"Who was your child's father?" The question came out harshly.

She blinked in surprise. *"What?"*

"Just answer."

"Why? Why do you care?"

She tried to pull back, but he held her there, much too close. Her breath still came out in little pants, but anxious ones now. What was he doing? Why was he asking her this now?

"*Brett.* Let go."

"Who was he?"

"His name was Rick. He was a hiker, lost. He spent a week, then left."

"Are you still in touch with him?"

"No."

"Did he contact you at all?"

"No."

"Did you love him?"

She stared at him incredulously. "What kind of question—"

"Never mind."

He released her abruptly and jerked to his feet with nervous raging energy.

A thrill shot through her. If her touch had meant nothing, he would have politely explained that he couldn't get involved and that would be it. He wouldn't have asked who Rick was and if she loved him. Which meant he felt it—he felt the same thing she did, and it made him just as crazy as it did her.

She got to her knees, ready to take him on, ready to confront him with what she knew and duke it out to its completion if necessary. She had every right. Why else would he be asking her all these questions if he didn't feel something for her?

Her stomach fell. Unless his questions meant he'd come here to get her help finding Rick.

"Is Rick in some kind of trouble?"

"How should I know?"

"Are you trying to find him?"

"No. I was sent to find you. I told you that."

She clenched her hands into fists even as she felt guilty relief. She didn't want to be talking about this now. She wanted to go back to being in his arms, feeling the contact, the peace, touching him, connecting. But she had a feeling the key was finally in her grasp and Pandora's box waited. She had to know.

"Who sent you to find me?"

"My sister."

"Shana."

"Yes."

"Why?"

He stopped his hobbling attempt at pacing, faced her with an expression of savage determination. "Because she wanted me to tell you instead of the police."

He was talking too fast and too loudly, gesturing with his hands. Layla unclenched her fists; her heart contracted. Something bad. Something very bad. She knew it by his hesitancy before this, by his anger now.

"She wanted you to tell me what?"

"Layla." His voice rose to a frustrated shout.

"Tell me." She rose to her feet. "Tell me now. I have a right to know, damn it."

"Phoebe isn't yours." The words exploded out of him. "The baby my sister has, her foster child, is your natural daughter. Phoebe isn't yours."

Layla heard the words. She heard every one of them. But as she stood there, staring at him, at his anger and his fear, not a single one made it far enough into her brain to register.

"What did you say?"

She sounded so calm. Except that she sounded calm and about a million miles away, and her heart had sped up to what felt like a dangerous, dangerous speed.

"Phoebe isn't yours, Layla. You have the wrong baby." His voice gentled into anguish. He barely got the words out.

"The wrong baby."

She was stupid now. Stupid. Repeating his sentences as if she had no mind of her own. "How can she be the wrong baby? She's *my* baby. I gave birth to her."

"No." He looked around the cabin, up, down, left,

right, anywhere but at her. "Someone switched her with yours. At the hospital."

"*Switched* her." She let out a hoarse laugh. From somewhere deep inside her, rage started flowing, creeping into her limbs and brain like a choking vine. "That is *ridiculous. You* are ridiculous. Who sent you to tell me bullshit like that?"

He looked at her then, directly into her eyes. She dropped hers immediately. She didn't want to look at him. Ever. The rage grew into a huge, frustrated need for action, for anything other than standing here being so damn calm. "How dare you come in here and spend all this time being nice to me as if you weren't about to try and tear my life apart with lies."

"Layla." He moved forward, tried to grab her arms. She shook him off and stepped back.

"Keep away from me." She sounded hysterical, breathless, crazy.

"I'm sorry." He held his hands up in surrender. "I didn't mean to tell you like this."

"Then why did you?" The cabin was suddenly hot, stifling, unbearably suffocating.

He took a deep breath. "I don't know. You got too close. I lost it. I don't know."

"You don't know." She mimicked him, cruel, raging, unable to control her fury. "To *hell* with you."

She ran for the door and grabbed her parka, shook him off when he tried to pursue her, and plunged out into the cold, open, infinite space that was blessedly free of Brett Devlin and his vicious empty words.

CHAPTER EIGHT

BRETT STOPPED HIMSELF from following and watched Layla disappear through the door. The same feeling. The same feeling he'd had as a boy of twelve when his grandfather's gold watch, a watch he'd inherited only a few months before, had slipped off his too small wrist and fallen into the pond down the road from Larry Boyd's house. That eerie, distorted experiencing of time and space and color.

The final brilliant flash of metal sinking into murky green; the last shadowy glimpse of Layla's form racing by the window into the night. The sick certainty he'd done something terribly wrong that he hadn't meant to, that pain and punishment were on the way.

Only this time he'd be punishing himself, waiting in this damn tiny cabin, feeling tinier all the time, while the woman he'd somehow come to care for was sitting out in the snow with her heart ripped open.

Geezus.

He curled his fingers into fists and pressed the fists against his forehead. The night after he'd lost Grandfather's watch, he'd lain in bed, backside stinging from the beating his mom had given him, teeth clenched, fists clenched, brain on fire with hatred he now recognized as guilt. He'd make them pay; he'd make them all pay.

Apparently everyone deserved to pay for what he'd done except him.

He opened his fists, dragged his palms down his face and tried to calm himself into his usual state of reason. But he couldn't shake the picture of that angry little boy, furious at life, furious at the raw deal he thought he'd gotten. Real father kicked out of the house, new father in the house, nothing good enough for his mother...

Everything had felt out of his control, and he'd detested the feeling with an intensity that had colored the rest of his life.

Out of control was exactly what he'd gotten when he put his arms around Layla as a brotherly gesture of comfort. The feel of her strong, slender body, resisting at first then curling into his as if she couldn't help herself, the feel of her soft hair against his jaw, the total shock of her soft lips on his neck had brought on an explosive, terrifying response.

Not just lust, though he was well aware of his attraction to her. Something deeper, something unexplainable, something he'd never felt before.

Mr. Brett Devlin, the consummate P.I., who stayed passive and unmoved in the face of danger, murder and unspeakable cruelty, had had the shit scared out of him by a beautiful, unexpectedly vulnerable hermit woman, and he'd reacted the same way he had as a boy. With anger, with the need to make her pay for something that was his own damn fault.

Well, he had made her pay. The words had come barreling out of him, designed to hurt her, to push her so far away she could never come close again.

He was no better now than he'd been at twelve.

Alycia stirred; he walked over to the crib and stared

at her tiny perfection, reached to smooth her un-smoothable hair.

It had taken him the rest of the summer to find the watch. Even back then he had the precise memory and eye for detail that served him so well in his career. Every chance he could sneak away, he'd rowed his little boat out into the middle of the pond to the exact spot and dived, over and over, groping along the muddy bottom until one heart-stopping day, his hand raked over cold metal links. He'd taken the watch home, told no one, let it dry and put it in a small box in his room.

He still had it, still in the same box. Maybe when he got home he'd dig that box out of whatever closet he'd stored it in and get the watch cleaned and work-ing again. Maybe he'd even start wearing it.

The baby stirred again; he touched her warm pink cheek and glanced at the dark outside. How long would Layla stay out there? Alycia would need her.

He glanced at the clock and moved away from the crib, hating himself, hating the thought of her out there alone with her grief in the dark cold night even more.

The tension built until he had to start pacing, bad ankle and all, ten feet one way, ten feet back. He glanced at the clock thirty seconds after he told him-self to stop glancing at it, swore not to glance any-more, then thirty seconds later glanced all over again.

Ten feet this way, ten feet that, ten feet this way, ten feet that, then two extra steps until he was right in front of the door. All summer long he'd looked for that watch. All summer long he'd gone after it with a single-minded determination to make it right, even if only he knew he'd done so.

All summer long.

Brett lunged for his jacket and yanked open the door. He wasn't just as bad as when he was twelve.

He was worse.

LAYLA HUDDLED DEEPER into her parka, each hand shoved into the opposite sleeve to make up for her lack of mittens. She didn't know how long she'd walked before she turned back, didn't know how far. All she knew was that she couldn't stay out here in her favorite clearing much longer. She'd had the presence of mind to grab her parka, but had been too desperate to escape to stop for her boots, and her sheepskin slippers were cold through. Suicide by idiocy-induced hypothermia wasn't her way of doing things.

Unfortunately, except for having to take care of Baby—Layla dug her nails into her palms under the parka sleeves—she didn't want to go back.

Going back meant facing Brett, meant facing facts, or lack of them, asking more questions, deciding whether to believe him, deciding what this might mean to her future, to her entire life…

She let her head drop forward, the swish of her nylon hood loud next to her ears in the relative silence of the woods. Her brain refused to consider the rest of her life right now. She needed to cope with an hour at a time. An hour at a time was how the rest of her life would go by anyway. She'd deal with each one as it—

Her head jerked up. Not a sound had alerted her, at least not consciously, but he was here. She could sense him, the same way she had at the height of the now-passed storm an eternity ago, when he'd been lying out here injured.

"Layla." His voice was back to gentle, not the harsh tone he'd used in the cabin before she'd fled.

She turned and saw him, a black human shape among tree trunks, white snow on the ground reflecting the glow of moonlight through thinning clouds. Why had he followed her? He must be cold out here, in pain. Did he think she was out to do herself harm? Or that she'd come to some harm in these woods that were her own backyard? What had possessed him?

He moved closer, and if a limp could look strong and reassuring and purposeful, his could. This tough Nebraska P.I., wearing a leather jacket and hiking boots, as if ready for a stroll across a springtime meadow.

Two days he'd been here. What an impossibly short time to have developed feelings this complex, only to have them threatened to be blown to hell by the message he'd come to deliver.

He hobbled forward until he stood two feet away, then he held out his hand, his breath audible in the stillness. "Come home."

Her heart twisted painfully. *Come home.* As if the cabin was their home together. Or as if he himself embodied home, standing wounded and proud with his hand outstretched.

"We need to talk about this."

Layla nodded wearily, the thrill dissipating. They did. They needed to talk about it. She needed to let herself think about it. She needed to nurse her beautiful daughter and open her mind to the horrible possibility that Baby was someone else's beautiful daughter. She needed to stop sitting on a stump in the middle of the freezing cold mountain woods and deal with all this as a rational adult.

She got up, ignoring Brett's hand, and headed back for the cabin, matching his pace. Only hours ago she'd been thinking he was sent here by God for her sexual deliverance. She snorted and stumbled on a snow-covered log. The sin of ego. Pride had gone before, and here was her fall.

They reached the cabin, stamped snow off their feet, filed inside and took off their jackets and footwear.

Layla walked slowly over to where Baby slept. She didn't want to face her. But her feet were drawn to the crib, like someone passing a horrendous wreck on the road who didn't want to see, absolutely didn't want to see, but had to turn to look, anyway.

One step at a time.

She reached the railing and clutched it, her safety on the deck of this pitching ship that had become her life.

"Are you supposed to take her?" Her voice broke. The idea of anyone taking her child away was ludicrous.

"No." He came up behind her, stood close enough that she could sense his warmth. "I was just supposed to find you and tell you."

"I see. Well, you did that."

"Yes." The raw pain in his voice made her almost wish she could take back her jab.

Baby slept, mouth puckered, cheeks a soft pink. Layla thought back to the hospital delivery room, the excitement, the anticipation, the intense vicious challenge of the normal pain of labor, then the uncontrollable agony and the certainty that something was horribly wrong. She was hemorrhaging. Bleeding uncontrollably. They wouldn't give her her baby. They had to do something to her, suction her lungs.

All the panic, all the pain, a blur of action and time, then blissful relief when they'd put her under for emergency surgery. Nothing after, but dreams of her baby girl. Then coming to, the struggle for consciousness and her first real gaze at the daughter they handed her, and she'd had to bite back the words, *I'm sorry, this isn't her.*

Had she known? Had she somehow instinctively known?

"How did they find my…the girl I gave birth to? How did they know she'd been switched?"

"A couple was involved in a car accident in Seattle." His voice turned impersonal, as if he were narrating an educational documentary. "They had a month-old infant with them who survived. The woman had given birth, but not to the baby with her. The Seattle police were unable to find the baby's birth mother, so after my sister, I'm sure, rammed my grossly exaggerated talent down their throats, they asked me to help find her."

"Me." She couldn't take her eyes off Baby. "Where is…the baby now?"

"Shana has her."

"Her foster child." She murmured the words slowly, as if she were drugged and barely functional. Her mind had to be turning off. Thoughts and logic and questions were more and more of a struggle to produce. "That's right. You told me."

"Yes."

A tiny ray of hope found its way into her fogged-up brain. In foster care. Not with loving parents. "Then the other mother…"

"She and her husband were killed in the accident."

"So this baby is an orphan. If her parents are dead, she's an orphan."

The ray of hope grew. If Baby's parents were dead, Layla could keep her. They wouldn't take her child away from her. They couldn't. "So I can keep her *and* my birth daughter—if the parents were killed."

"Layla."

If she thought his voice had shown the maximum amount of pain it could show already, she was wrong.

She could feel herself withdrawing, closing off from her emotions as if some internal switch had been thrown. They were going to take Baby away. She knew it. The authorities, the system—they'd been against people like her from the beginning. Why should it be any different now? Why should they care about this crazy woman who lived by herself? *Take the kid away. Give her her own back, she'll be fine.*

"No relatives of the deceased couple could be found, so the baby went into foster care." He took a deep breath. Layla listened, waited, as if she were in some other dimension watching all this pain happen to someone else.

"But the child's uncle recently materialized. He and his wife want the child. Very much."

"Her name is Phoebe, not 'the child.'"

Brett put his hands on her shoulders, moved his thumbs in a massaging caress over her rock-tense muscles. "You gave the name Phoebe to your birth daughter. According to the hospital birth records, this child's name is Alycia."

"Alycia." Layla laughed, a brittle scared sound. "I never called her anything but 'Baby.'"

She put her hand to her mouth to cut off any more of the horrible hysterical giggles. Had she really known deep down that Baby wasn't hers? Was that why she hadn't bonded with the infant as deeply as she'd expected to?

Or when faced with this other baby they said was her "real" daughter, would she still struggle, still feel that something was missing? Was she even capable of feeling that kind of deep love?

What kind of woman rejected all her own species, felt the passion and pull of sexual attraction and the mild infatuation that went with it, but nothing more?

This was her worst nightmare come true. And she'd thought Brett had held up a mirror to reflect the worst of herself. This new baby could shatter her completely. It seemed life had devised the most crushing brutal test possible for a woman who felt that life had already tested her plenty.

How much longer could she go on rationalizing that what wouldn't kill her would make her stronger? How much stronger did she really need to be?

"If it makes you feel any better, the officer in charge of the investigation has met Alycia's uncle and said he seems like a really good person. He recently moved back to the States from France, he's newly married, well-off, and he and his wife love children."

"He wants his niece."

"He and his wife want to adopt her, yes. They can't have children of their own."

"I see."

She was going to have to give Baby up. Even if she had the money to fight, she'd never win. If this uncle had lived abroad, he was probably cultured, educated, and Brett said he was wealthy—everything she wasn't. She'd never win.

"And your Phoebe needs you, Layla." His thumbs

stopped moving and he squeezed her shoulders, moved forward until his chest made contact with her back and his chin rested against her hair. "Shana's taken good care of her, but you're her mother. She belongs with you."

Layla flinched, not taking a shred of comfort from his strong presence. This was her daughter in the crib in front of her. She didn't know that other child. Those feelings in the hospital couldn't have been real. *I'm sorry, this isn't her.* How could she possibly have known what her daughter would look like? She'd never even seen her.

"How did the switch happen? How *could* it happen? All those nurses…the ID bracelets…"

Her voice sounded flat and oddly distant. Someone was taking this crushing news awfully calmly. She was the child's mother, the baby had drunk milk from her breast its whole life. Shouldn't she be sobbing? Screaming? After that initial flood of rage at Brett, she felt nothing.

Maybe that was all she was capable of feeling.

"I don't know. But it did happen. The police will be able to tell you better than I can, though even they'll be going on theory. We'll probably never know exactly."

Layla released her death grip on the crib railing and turned away from Baby, away from his hands on her shoulders. She didn't want to look any more. Didn't want to be touched or watched or spoken to.

She felt the same way she'd felt when she found her parents dead. As if something had simply shut off inside her. After the initial shock of discovering the bodies, she hadn't wanted to look any more. She hadn't shed a tear, then or since. She'd calmly walked out of the tiny house they'd rented with two other families, found a pay phone, called 9-1-1 and told the sweet-voiced lady on the line that her parents were dead. Then she'd hung up and kept walking until a police cruiser found her and brought her in.

She'd felt that same shut-off way until Baby came into her life, when a little thaw had begun.

And then Brett showed up and the thaw had become a trickle, threatening to gush into a stream. Now she'd frozen up again, solid and safe.

Fine by her. It was so much easier to feel nothing. Easier and more natural to her.

Her footsteps sounded unusually heavy and quick as she walked over to the woodstove and added a few logs from her dwindling supply to the dying fire. Her senses seemed to be on hyper-alert. Sounds were too loud, the fire was too bright, the wood seemed especially heavy and rough.

She'd have to remember to get more from the supply shed on her next trip out. Luckily she'd learned by now to chop enough in the fall to last her the entire winter.

The chore was odious enough when the weather was fine. In winter, she'd learned the hard way, it was a whole lot more odious.

Last year, though, at Patson's Hardware, she'd found a new device to split the logs that got the job done in a fraction of the time and with far greater accuracy. Great hardware store.

She swore they had everything on earth. She loved going there to stare at the neatly arranged boxes of nails and screws and bolts and hooks and fasteners and hardware of all shapes and—

Baby let out a wail from her crib that made Layla

jump and nearly topple over from her crouch on the floor. She carefully closed and latched the door on the stove, checking it twice before she moved to the crib and picked Baby up, aware of Brett's eyes on her.

Leave me alone, leave me alone. She didn't want to see pity or speculation about why she wasn't reacting more to the news. If he thought she was an unfeeling robot, that was his prerogative. It probably wasn't far from the truth.

She brought the warm, squalling bundle to her rocker, sat and lifted her shirt, let the tiny mouth fasten on her nipple and suck. She rocked the same rhythm as always, kept her eyes ahead, gazing at the decorative bunch of dried reddish-brown chilis she'd hung from her kitchen ceiling, gazing at the copper pot she'd found at a yard sale outside Leavenworth and brought home to polish and display, gazing at the scratch on one of the cabinets she kept meaning to fix, humming, rocking, nursing.

"Layla."

She turned at the hoarse sound of his voice to find Brett watching her as if he expected her to spontaneously combust any second, his jaw set, fists clenched at his sides.

"What is it?"

She interrupted her humming to speak, then started in again, an aimless tune that didn't sound like any song she'd ever heard. What was *he* so upset about?

"I'm sorry."

"About what?" She eyed him calmly. The poor guy looked as if he was about to freak?

"I'm sorry I told you the way I did."

She shrugged. "You did what you had to do. It's

not like it would have been different news if it came
out gently.''

He stared at her for a few more seconds. A mass of
anger and impatience started in her chest. She turned
away from him, went back to her humming, went back
to staring at the familiar comforting objects in her
kitchen.

Honestly, you'd think he'd been told to give up his
own baby.

The idea was so absurd, she started to giggle. Which
made Baby do a little up-and-down shaky dance at her
breast, which made her giggle even harder.

Brett came forward faster than she'd seen him move
since he tried to dodge her bullet in the woods. Kneeling in front of her on the floor, he gripped the sides
of her thighs in his large strong hands and stared ear-
nestly up at her with so much tender concern she
wanted to scream at him to leave her alone. ''It's going to be okay.''

She shrugged again and wiped away the tears of
laughter with the hand not holding Baby. ''Of course
it is. It's wonderful. I'll get my *real* baby back. One
big, super-duper, happy family reunion.''

''Stop it.'' He gripped her harder and she had the
impression he wanted to slug her as much as she
wanted to slug him. Maybe it would do them both
good.

''Stop what?'' She looked at him innocently. If he
thought she was going to play the bereaved anguished
mother just for his benefit, he had much more thinking
to do.

His grip on her thighs loosened; he moved away,
still watching her intently. ''Nothing. We can talk
about it tomorrow.''

"Tomorrow would be just swell." She let Baby finish nursing, burped her, changed her into a fresh diaper and her pajamas with clumsy jerky movements, and plunked her in her infant carrier before she fished around in the wooden toy chest she'd made for a new set of distractions to hang over the seat.

There. All set.

She reached her arms overhead, muscles lengthening, stretching, then starting to shake. She yanked her arms down. Enough of that. Her bed looked smooth and inviting. Right now she wanted to change into her sweats, lie down and read for a couple of hours before Baby needed more food and went down for the night.

Brett could do whatever the hell he pleased. No cozy fireside chats with Beaujolais tonight.

That part of their relationship was over.

CHAPTER NINE

BRETT ROUSED HIMSELF from sleep with an effort. The baby was wailing. Strange, Layla hadn't tended to her. Not like her.

He rolled over on the sofa and dragged his eyes open. The wailing continued, low and eerie, not like any noise he'd heard the baby make before.

He lifted up onto his elbows to register the sound better.

Oh, God.

It was Layla.

He threw off the sleeping bag, lit the kerosene lamp she'd put on the end table next to the couch, and limped over to her bed. She lay there, eyes open and staring, moaning sobs rising from her throat.

"Layla."

She didn't answer, didn't move, didn't stop the chilling noises of grief.

"Layla." He touched her shoulder. "Are you okay?"

She turned and looked up, tear trails glistening on her cheeks, her eyes strangely glassy, not quite making contact with his, even though she was staring right at him. "Yes. I'm fine."

He put the lamp carefully on her bedside table and felt her forehead. Cool. Not feverish.

"Do you know what day it is?"

"Yes."

"What?"

"I don't—" She frowned. "Wood is going."

He sat next to her on the bed, vastly relieved. She was still asleep. Shana had been a sleepwalker for years and had often come into his room, so he recognized the look and the confusion.

"It's okay, Layla."

"I'm not— I don't—" She shook her head.

"Shh-hhh." He stroked her cheek, his heart aching. It was killing him that this proud closed-off woman could only cry in her sleep. He was one to talk, but he knew she needed to let these emotions out to be able to process them.

He had a fierce, completely lunatic urge to be the one to make it safe for her to feel openly. To cry in his arms if she needed to. To grieve the loss of her child in a normal healthy way.

"You're fine, sweetheart. Go back to sleep."

She turned immediately, like a small child obeying her parent, and nestled back into the covers, eyes closed, breathing peacefully.

He stayed beside her…why? In case she cried again. In case she woke for real. In case she needed him, even though she probably wouldn't let herself.

He stayed because he couldn't leave. Because the sight of her face relaxed in sleep, cheeks damp, hair in disarray on the pillow kept him here. Because he wanted to touch her, to slip under the covers with her, to feel her body pressed against his so he could protect her physically right here, right now.

Because he wanted to fight the world to keep it from hurting her any more than it already had. If Jim and Patty Lehr, who'd snatched her child before they'd known if their own was healthy or not, weren't already dead, he'd want to see them suffer for their selfishness the same way Layla would have to.

Layla stirred, whimpered, let out a moan of grief. Brett winced and reached to touch her face. Granted, the Lehrs had set up the circumstances that had brought him here, but that didn't stop him from feeling as if he'd done this to her, as if he was responsible for this new pain in her life, because he'd been the one to tell her.

He leaned over and blew out the lamp, slid into the bed as quietly and carefully as he could and pulled her into his arms. If she let him, he'd do as damn much as he possibly could to help her through this.

If not—he smiled and nuzzled her hair—at least her gun wasn't in easy reach of the bed.

LAYLA BURROWED UP from a deep sleep. Something was different. She was warmer. Too warm. Confined. Something was keeping her from moving.

Trapped. She was trapped.

She lashed out with arms and legs and heard an annoyed male grunt.

Brett.

She hurled herself away from his dark shape, up on her elbows, panting.

In her *bed.*

"What are you doing here?"

The last sound she expected came out of his mouth. Laughter. He was laughing.

Her fear turned to bewilderment, then annoyance. "*What* is so funny?"

"You." He got his chuckles under control and took a deep breath. "You are so funny. It was either laugh or sock you back or... God, I don't know, something had to give."

Layla thrust a hand through her hair. This was surreal. She'd finally gone to sleep, had horrible wrenching nightmares about being forced to put Baby in the path of an oncoming train, and woken up to a man in her bed who thought she was God's gift to comedy.

"*What* are you doing in my bed?"

"You were crying in your sleep." His voice held no more traces of laughter; he sounded gentle and protective.

The annoyance drained out of her. She sat forward and touched her fingers to her eyes. Her lashes were still wet. She sometimes woke up this way in the middle of the night, aware she'd been crying.

"I had...some bad dreams."

"I figured."

He made no move to get out of her bed. And because she was still spooked by her dreams and by waking in a panic, and because he was strong and calm and reassuring, she didn't insist he did, though she undoubtedly should have.

Something about having him here with her, something about the darkness and the utterly normal feeling of her cabin at night, made the situation with Baby seem far away, as if it wasn't really happening, as if it wouldn't exist again until the sun came up.

The feeling was a tremendous relief.

"What was so funny?"

He cleared his throat and she heard him moving on the bed, as if he was uncomfortable with what he had to say.

"What? Did I talk in my sleep? Say something crazy?"

"No."

She frowned and peered toward him. The coals from the night's fire glowed orange behind the glass of the woodstove door but didn't give off enough light to see his face clearly.

"I had this...image or...fantasy that didn't quite work out. In retrospect, it was pretty funny."

Her startled intake of breath sounded much too loud in the silent room.

"A fantasy?" The words came out breathless and intrigued, which wasn't how she'd meant them to at all. "About me?"

Even more incredible, her body was slowly becoming aware of him here beside her in the darkness, in an entirely female manner. How could this be happening? Her life was about to be smashed into pulp and she dealt with it by getting horny?

He moved again; she couldn't tell what or where, but the covers made a soft swish and the bed jarred beneath her.

"You were crying in your sleep. I wanted to...reassure you. It seemed a good idea at the time."

"Oh. I see." No, she didn't. *That* was his fantasy? To reassure her?

She wanted to ask more, but asking more would make her seem too persistent, obviously fishing for what she hoped this fantasy of his would be. Asking more would give away the fact that the warmth in her body was growing warmer.

"I imagined—I fantasized—that you'd wake up and...turn to me for comfort."

"Oh." She held her breath. Was there more?

He must have gestured with his arm because she felt it drop down beside her on the mattress. "But of course, you, being Layla, gave me possible internal injuries instead.''

She couldn't help smiling. "Sorry to disappoint you.''

"Oh, no.'' His voice was mischievous and strangely tender. "You've never even come close to doing that.''

Her breath caught in her throat. She lay back down on the pillow beside him and blinked up at the ceiling she could barely see. Her body was sending her crazy insistent hormonal signals that seemed out of place and embarrassing in the circumstances. He was being a good friend. A caring person who'd wanted her to be able to turn to him in her time of need. How could she be feeling like this? Not merely aroused, but wildly so, desperately so.

"Brett.'' She whispered his name.

"Yes.''

"Was that…the whole fantasy?''

She heard his breath go in, heard his head lift off the pillow and turn toward her. "Did you want there to be more, Layla?''

"I…yes.''

She whispered again into the darkness, felt the thrill of her own daring, the warmth spreading downward, the way paper charred yellow, then brown, before it burst into flame. She wanted him. She wanted him insanely. She wanted to spend her energy and her pain and her every emotion making love with him. Lose herself in it so that nothing else mattered or existed.

"Is there something you'd like to happen?'' He was whispering, too, as if even in this tiny cabin in the middle of nowhere, he needed to make the space more intimate, until it only had room for the two of them. "Right now?"

"Yes."

"Tell me."

"I'd like…I need…" She shifted on the bed, her breath coming in tiny pants.

"You need something from me?"

"Yes." She didn't move except to form the word. He knew what she meant. He knew. He felt it the same as she did. "I need *you*."

He reached out, brushing his hand along the pillow until he found her hair and stroked it. "Are you sure?"

"Yes." Her body was still heating, nearly catching fire. "It would help me."

His hand stilled on her hair. "Help you?"

"I need a release for all this." Her voice broke, pleaded, even as she tried to keep it calm. "All this…upheaval."

"That's all you—" He cut himself off abruptly; his hand grew heavy on her head.

She held her breath. *Please, please don't say no.*

"Okay."

Her breath let itself out on a soft "Oh" of pleasure.

"If you're sure."

"I'm sure."

He moved forward, toward her; she waited, the wait electric and thrilling. His lips found her forehead and lingered, a warm, slow kiss that mixed her arousal with a huge dose of relief. *Thank you.*

She wrapped her arms around his broad shoulders, pressed her body to his warmth, aware in one corner of her one-track mind that it felt good to lean against someone, to let him share the weight of her body and the weight in her heart.

He kissed her forehead again, moved his mouth down to her cheek, to the corner of her mouth—warm, soft kisses—then pulled back just enough so his lips hovered right over hers and hers tingled in anticipation.

"You're *sure* you're sure?"

"*Brett.*" She was going to kill him.

He chuckled and took her face in his hands, his voice husky and low. "I was teasing. There's no way in hell I'm letting you back out now, and possibly not ever."

Not ever? What did he mean by that? "What—"

He moved close again and touched his mouth to hers, kissed her gently, sweetly, and her brain turned off to everything but the warm taste of his lips.

"*Oh*, that's so nice." Her words came out on a soft, breathy groan.

"Mmm." He gathered her closer, if that was even possible, and kissed her harder, thoroughly, a long slow kiss that made her want to throw back her head and say, "Oh Brett" afterward, which she always thought was the most ridiculous crock when she saw it in the movies.

But, oh, the way this man could kiss.

He kissed her again, and again, and again and again. After a while the kisses started traveling from her mouth down to her heart, and through the rest of her, turning her into a dizzy, breathless, ridiculous excuse of a person who didn't want to do anything more for the rest of her life but kiss this man in this bed.

This wasn't at all what she expected, wasn't at all what she wanted. She wanted lust, frenzy, quick and hard and dirty.

The emotion, the sensation, built and built, forcing

her to respond more and more deeply until she broke the kiss, before she relinquished her emotional control entirely. She couldn't handle this much feeling. Not this way.

She wrapped her leg around his hip to bring him closer and pushed rhythmically against his erection, grinding, enticing, blatantly sexual. This was much easier, to lie back and let her body's needs take over, to make sure he understood what it was she was after.

"Hey." He spoke gently, pulled her arms from around his neck and pinned them with one hand to the pillow above her head. "What's your hurry?"

"I'm…hot." She moved her hips anxiously back toward him.

"I see." He trailed his other hand down to her waist and back up under her sweatshirt. "Hmm, so you are. Yes."

He dragged the last word out, as slow and sexy as the trip his hand was taking across her waist up to her breasts: *Ye-e-e-es.*

"Oh."

The noise broke from her mouth, guttural, gasping, and she pressed her lips together abruptly. She'd never made a sound during sex, always found it embarrassing even to want to, but it was beyond her to hold it in.

He released her hands, pulled her sweatshirt up and over her head, then moved over her on his hands and knees. He bent to kiss her mouth again, her throat, down to her breasts, sensitive in the chilly air of the cabin.

His mouth was warm, wet, and her breasts swelled shamelessly; she arched her back to him, inviting every lick, every touch.

"You like that?"

"Oh-hh, yes."

She wanted to laugh at how she sounded—drugged, dreamy, a sensual stranger.

He kissed her stomach, moved lower, lower still, pushing the thick material of her sweats down and out of the way. She inhaled endlessly, waiting, anticipating, half embarrassed, half on fire with longing.

Before Rick there had only been Pedro back in California, a fumbling, awkward mutual deflowering and a few times after, not much better. Rick had been lovely.

But this. This was way beyond lovely.

His tongue settled on her; she cried out at the sensation, clamped her hand to her mouth before she embarrassed him with her noise.

"No censorship." His strong arm reached up to move her hand away. "I want to hear you. I want to hear everything."

He went back to pleasuring her, more and more intensely. She tried to hold in her cries, gasps, animal panting sounds.

Forget it. He was making her crazy. She threaded her hands through his hair and gave in, grunting, moaning, kicking to free herself of her sweatpants, then gyrating her hips, pleading with him to send her over the top.

To her horror, he stopped, then got off the bed. "Wait here."

She froze. Where was he going? Had she disgusted him? She sat up. "Brett?"

He came back quickly. "Condom."

"Oh, thank goodness. I thought I—"

"What?" The crinkly package noise stopped. "You think I would have left if I didn't absolutely have to?"

"I don't know."

He chuckled, and she heard the snap of latex, then his dark shape came close and pushed her back on the bed. "Has anyone ever told you that you are unbelievably sexy?"

"No." She answered truthfully, then wished she hadn't when it sounded sort of pathetic.

"And all the more sexy for being totally unaware of it?"

"I don't. I mean, I don't know."

She glowed with pleasure, she was sure. If she looked down at herself right now, she'd be a soft, brilliant orange, lighting up the room.

"Take it from me." He kissed her twice, lingering, lovely kisses, then pulled his T-shirt over his head and lay over her again. "You are beautiful and very sexy. When you haven't been driving me crazy, you've been driving me wild. And any man who hasn't told you that should have his head examined."

"Oh."

She smiled in the dark and wrapped her arms around him, holding him close. He lay there, between her legs, his breathing hard and irregular.

"Layla."

She swallowed. This was going to get intense, and she didn't want intense. "Yes?"

"It will all be okay." His voice broke slightly; he seemed to have trouble forming his next words. "I'm here for you."

Something very strong and frightening and wonderful and threatening started growing in her.

"Thank you."

She clutched him to her, her body screaming with tension. If she didn't do something soon, she was going to cry hysterical buckets all over him and beg him to stay with her forever, and she had a feeling that once she started, she wasn't going to be able to stop.

"Make love to me, Brett."

His body stiffened briefly on top of her, then relaxed all at once, as if he'd forced himself to do it. "Yes."

He lifted himself up and pressed between her legs. She opened for him eagerly, coming alive with flame as he slid inside her, making herself concentrate on experiencing the physical sensation, sacrificing the emotional.

The physical was enough. It was all she could take right now.

He stroked her, slowly at first, building her back up toward her climax, then harder and faster, as if he knew she was getting close.

She urged him on, panting and kneading at his back, pressing his hips more firmly into hers, determined to disappear into the erotic sensation so there would be no more awareness of Brett, but simply an awareness of her body's needs and how they would be satisfied.

He responded as if he understood what she wanted from him, driving into her again and again until she burst over the edge, crying out, clutching his shoulders, pouring her grief and fear into the ultimate satisfaction of lust, straining to hold on to the peak as long as her body would allow it.

Then she came down, slowly, pressing her cheek to his for one fierce, tender moment before she pulled away, panting still, and enjoying the aftershock contractions between them, like random electrical bursts after a lightning strike.

Lust was all it could be right now. Lust was all she had room for.

CHAPTER TEN

BRETT WOKE to the feel of Layla's body nestled close to his, keeping him warm in the prefire chill of the cabin.

He lifted his head to look down at her, hair spilled across his chest, arms and legs sprawled over him. He moved a lock of hair that had fallen across her eyes, resisted the urge to stroke it back across her temple in case he woke her. She needed as much sleep as she could get. The light was just starting to filter in around the dark green window shades; Alycia would be waking, and all too soon Layla would have to get up and feed her. And deal with reality again.

He let his head fall back on the pillow, stared up at the pattern of dark knots in the aged golden pine, anticipating the loss of her warmth, the loss of the intimacy. She'd turned to him with animal passion last night, desperate for sexual release. She hadn't been making love to him, but to a handy male body that attracted her, one that let her get out some of her grief and rage when she couldn't allow herself to do it any other way.

Who knew what state she'd be in today? Would she need him again? Would she need him to stay away? Would she wake up and hold him closer or wake up and slug him in the gut?

His grin faded quickly. Last night…something had

started happening to him the minute he slid inside her. Along with the usual rush of erotic sensation had come a deep awareness of the woman he was with. Not just as a female, not just as someone turning on his body, but as someone turning on his heart.

The experience had shaken him, so that when he realized she wanted nothing more than a quick, hard coupling, he'd given it to her, to satisfy her need, and to save his own soul.

She might have been screwing a handy male body, but he'd been making love to her.

He closed his eyes and shook his head. God, was he sounding sappy. And Brett Devlin didn't ever sound sappy. Layla might have found her way under his skin, into his heart, but she couldn't take up residence there. They couldn't stay here, in this suspension of reality, much longer. The storm had passed over twenty-four hours ago. The plows would come; he'd call a tow truck this morning, go home to Nebraska and take on his next case.

Layla would have to take Alycia to Seattle, go through whatever legal maneuvering it would take to let Bruce Lehr adopt his niece. She'd get her birth child from Shana and start the new chapter of her life as a mom over again.

He had no place in this woman's home on top of this mountain, and she had no place in his.

The thought was meant to shake him back to take-charge reality, to get him out of this useless wistful mooning state. Instead, it sank him to a low he hadn't felt in years. Hadn't let himself feel in years.

He gave a dry chuckle. He and Layla were a pair, making such a tremendous effort not to allow themselves to feel anything. Control freaks, both of them.

Maybe this little interlude would teach them something about how important making peanut-butter sandwiches really wasn't.

Except that she hadn't yet dealt with the shock and grief of his blunt and badly timed announcement. After her first rage of denial, she'd simply shut down. That couldn't last forever. No one was that strong. Brett didn't have kids, but too many times he'd seen what losing them did to parents. What even the threat of losing them did. Layla had a tough, tough road ahead. Giving this child up, even to a loving relative... adjusting to a strange infant...

The thought came to him, instant, inevitable, intense and unwelcome. He wouldn't be there to help her through it.

And God help him, he wanted to be.

BABY WAS CRYING. Layla burrowed closer to Brett. *No, no, no.* She didn't want to wake up. She didn't want consciousness mucking up this wonderful feeling. Didn't want reality intruding. There would be too much to face today, too many emotions to have to process. Her. Baby. Brett. It was all too much. She wanted to lie here forever, suspended between sleeping and awake, savoring the comforting protective strength of the man beside her and push everything else away.

"Hey." Brett stirred, brushing the hair out of her face. "Your alarm went off."

"I know." She sighed and slid away from him, out of bed, the cold air in the cabin doing its best to make the journey as shocking and unpleasant as possible.

She wrapped her arms over her naked chest, all the colder for the warmth she'd just left, prickling with resentment Baby didn't deserve. The child needed food. She knew nothing about what was going on, what would happen to her.

Layla swallowed fiercely and picked her up. She glanced at the rocker distastefully and made a split-second decision. Forget that. She walked back to the bed, Baby nuzzling eagerly at her breasts, smelling the milk already.

Brett lifted the covers so she could slip in easily, then pulled them up over her and Baby. She lay on her side, facing him, wrapped Baby in the crook of her arm and helped her latch on.

She could feel Brett watching them, hear him swallow suddenly in the silence. She laid her head on the pillow, feeling the tiny sucking mouth doing its work, emptying her mind of the significance of the moment. She wouldn't think past this minute, then the next, then the next.

This wasn't her child. She would manage. This wasn't her man. She would manage. She'd chosen this life because this life was what she wanted. She'd chosen to go through with the pregnancy, because a baby was what she'd wanted. She could still have both those things. The same life here, only without Brett. And a baby, only not this one.

Brett put his arm around her waist under the covers, reached forward and kissed her forehead.

"Don't." She pulled back from him, from the warmth and rightness of the family feeling, from the tears that were going to come crashing in if he kept that up.

He moved away, which only made her miss his closeness. He didn't seem at all upset, as if he understood what she needed and why. "Sorry about that."

Baby stopped sucking and turned toward the sound of his voice.

"Hi, there." He smiled down at her. "Not used to having me in bed, too?"

Baby stared at him for a second, then her features spread into a face-consuming grin before she turned back and resumed suckling.

Brett chuckled. "Guess she's not offended."

"I guess." She stared at the top of Baby's head, at the soft spot in the skull covered with thin fluffy hair that pulsed in rhythm with her sucking, then fixed her eyes on a blue patch in her wedding ring quilt.

She didn't want to look at Baby, didn't want to think about what had to happen. She didn't want to look at Brett, either. She didn't want any acknowledgment of the intimate family trio or what happened between them last night that went way beyond sex. Didn't want to see his eyes soften, didn't want hers to. This was temporary. The more she indulged the feelings, the harder they'd be to let go.

She closed her eyes. Last night had been necessary; if she hadn't been able to find some release sexually, she would have had to find it sobbing, and that would have helped no one. But something had gone wrong, something had backfired. She'd found her release, yes. But before he'd even been inside her, before she'd been able to push the emotions away and only feel with her body, had come all those beautiful and scary feelings of longing, of her insides shifting and enlarging to include him inside her heart.

Allowing those feelings or encouraging them was emotional suicide. She couldn't forget the weeks of miserable emptiness after Rick had left. Having this man leave would be ten times worse. Possibly a hundred. Not just because this time she'd be left having to exchange her child with a strange one that was also supposed to be hers. But simply because she'd be without him.

The next lost hiker that came by her cabin, she was just going to shoot and be done with it.

"You okay?"

She opened her eyes, feeling dull and empty already. "Sure. Fine."

He frowned slightly. "We should talk about what is going to happen."

"Yes." The warmth of the moment evaporated. She felt herself shutting down again.

"You think the plows will be here today?"

"Probably." She broke Baby's hold on her breast and sat up to burp her.

"Okay. I'll call a tow truck to get my pickup out of your woods. I'll also call my sister and let her know I've told you and that you are okay."

"Good."

"Another thing?"

"Yes?" Sure. Whatever.

"Can Shana let Bruce Lehr know that you'll agree to let him adopt his niece?"

She felt the tension stiffen her face; felt her eyes go hard and glassy. A muscle jumped in her cheek, absurdly out of her control.

"Yes." She sounded like a mechanical being, like a Layla-bot. "He should have his niece."

"Okay." His voice was thick with emotion.

She felt a swelling of anger and impatience. "Whatever."

Immediately, Brett got out of bed and pulled on his clothes, probably sensing, as usual, what she needed—

for him and his emotions and his gratitude to get the hell away from her. "I'll also need to talk to Jaron Dorsey, who headed the investigation into the mystery baby, and find out what steps we need to take—how soon you'll have to go to Seattle, etcetera."

"Okay." She thumped Baby's back in the practiced rhythm, starting at the lower back and moving upward, thump-thump, coaxing the gas out before it could settle painfully into her tiny intestines and make everyone miserable.

The routine task helped ease her paralysis, helped coax her back to a more normal feel. The passion of last night and the warm waking into intimacy were over. She'd file them carefully away for her worst lonely moments.

This morning, the events that were going to redefine her life were starting.

Baby chose to punctuate that thought with a hearty belch. Brett chuckled and came to stand by the bed, looking down at them. "She'll always be the champ."

"Yes. She's gifted. Her uncle will be blessed."

Brett chuckled again, then to her surprise, he sat on the bed and took her hand, gazing down at it as if fingers fascinated him. "It's going to be okay, Layla."

She tensed and took back her hand. "You keep saying that."

He brought those keen eyes up to hers. "Because I know it's true and I don't think you do."

She handed Baby to him and got up, pulling on her clothes with furious, fumbling movements. "I'm going to be fine. I just have to get to Seattle, give my child away, get my child back, and everything will be nifty."

She finished dressing, went over to the fireplace and

crouched to get a blaze going. He was right. She didn't think it was going to be in the slightest bit okay. She'd lived up here for eight years on her own; she'd have to drive by herself to a major city, subject herself to unfamiliar surroundings, crowds, and more scrutiny from people she didn't know, who would think she was peculiar.

Brett's sister would pretend to want to hear all about her life, would pity her and fuss over her. All those strangers staring with sick fascination as she handed over this child she'd thought was her own flesh and blood, watching while she accepted a new child, *her* child, who would be a total stranger. A child who wouldn't know the taste of her milk or the smell of her body.

Under the microscope of humanity at the most vulnerable moment, with no defense.

Not to mention having to get used to this other Phoebe, to her routines and moods and temperament.

Not to mention living in this cabin for the rest of her life with the memories of how it felt and sounded and smelled to have *him* here. In her room, in her bed, in her arms.

He had no idea how not "okay" she was.

She got the fire going, burned herself shoving a piece of dropped kindling into the blaze and shot to her feet, nursing her finger.

Breakfast. Breakfast came next. Hot cereal with apricots and raisins served in white bowls with a lupin pattern.

She turned to go to the kitchen and found Brett standing in her way. Baby was in her seat. She pushed past him; she didn't want sympathy, didn't want any false reassurances.

He grabbed her arm, brought her around to face him. "I'm not leaving you to face this by yourself, Layla. I'll drive you to Seattle, then back here to make sure you and the baby get through this."

She pulled herself up rigidly, wanting to scream, feeling torn in two. Part of her desperately wanted to accept. Desperately wanted him there. Someone she knew and had come to trust. Someone she cared for despite herself. Someone who could be on her side against the unknown hordes. Someone who could watch out for her and get her through this.

But then what? How long would all that take? A month? Two? Six? Who knew how long the courts would take, or how complicated the legal issues would be. How deep were her feelings for him after two damn days? How much deeper would they be after so much more time? Especially when she was at her most vulnerable. Especially with him there to protect her. All her prized independence, all her determination to live freely, without hurt and entanglement—all were in danger.

Watching him leave today would crack her heart. Watching him leave after going through such a deeply emotional experience with him at her side would pulverize it.

"Thank you, Brett. But I need to do this by myself."

He gave her an incredulous glare. "Layla, for God's sake, even the Incredible Hulk isn't tough enough to do something like this by himself. You'll need me there."

She managed a look of scorn, which she didn't feel. "I don't *need* anyone."

"Okay." He took a patient breath. "Then maybe you'll *want* me there."

She gave herself away. A convulsive swallow and a quick intake of breath that sounded like a sob.

"I can't let you do this." Her voice came out uneven and low.

"Why?"

She breathed out. In. Quick ragged puffs. "I'm sure you have things to do. I'm sure you have..." She gestured helplessly.

He drew her close, kissed her forehead, her cheeks and her mouth. "I want to do this. I can't stand for you to go through this alone."

She let herself melt against him, to savor the feel of his strong arms around her. It was so tempting. God, it was so tempting.

Baby let out a shriek; Layla and Brett swung around immediately to find her looking extremely pleased with herself.

She shrieked again, and gave her dangling toys a wide, toothless grin.

Layla clenched her jaw and felt Brett's hands closing over her tight fists, his body close behind her. "I don't have a reputation for going out of my way for people, Layla. In fact, the opposite. My sister tells me I'm an antisocial, self-absorbed, uncaring monster."

She laughed in spite of herself. "I think that's generally seen as my label."

"We can share. Agreed?"

Layla nodded and managed another smile. "Agreed."

"But for some reason, God help me, I want to help you." He moved his hands up to her shoulders, stroked the tight muscles there and at the base of her neck. "Last night—"

His hands stilled on her body. Layla turned her head to the side, listening intently. The noise was unmistakable. A powerful motor, a scraping shovel. She was suddenly desperate to know what he'd been about to say.

"Last night?"

His hands dropped from her shoulders, leaving her feeling cold and abandoned.

"The plow's here." He walked over to the bed and rummaged in his jacket. "I have to make those calls."

CHAPTER ELEVEN

LAYLA STUCK THE PLASTIC key card into the lock of Room 109 at the least expensive hotel she could find in Pioneer Square, downtown Seattle until the blinking green light went on. She pushed the door open, Alycia heavy in the backpack carrier, suitcase and diaper bag and infant seat heavy on her arm.

The door swung open into a stale-smelling, chilly, silent room. A king-size bed took up half the space; the overly smiley lady at the desk said they'd send up a crib for Alycia.

The door closed behind Layla with a loud thunk that startled Alycia into crying.

Layla didn't blame her.

She put down her battered suitcase, the fancy blue-flowered diaper bag she'd bought at a garage sale while pregnant and used all of twice, and the infant seat, then carefully sat, making certain the backpack was steady on the floor before she wriggled out of the straps and lifted Alycia into her arms.

She was amazed at how quickly she'd started to think of the child as Alycia. Amazed at how quickly she'd detached, so that she now thought of herself as a sitter instead of the child's mother.

That couldn't be natural. She had to be some seriously cold freak to be able to turn her back that quickly on the child she'd raised since birth.

Alycia stopped crying; Layla took off her tiny coat and her own and set the baby in her seat. She crossed to the window temperature control unit and fiddled with the buttons and dial until a deafening blast of hot air burst out and started warming the room.

The drive here had been fairly effortless. She was a good navigator, and the directions Brett had gotten from his sister had been clear, the weather cooperative and the traffic light.

She was doing fine. She'd even felt a little thrill of excitement coming into the city, as if part of her missed all the reasons she'd escaped to her mountain. Leavenworth was so familiar now, she didn't notice it much. Did her errands, nodded, smiled, chatted when necessary. Every time she went there, she focused on her errands, her supplies, her pottery.

But this city had nothing of the familiar; in many ways she was as anonymous and isolated here as she was on the mountain. Which was why she had declined Shana's offer to stay with her at Keith's town house and had checked into this hotel instead. The room wasn't so bad now that it was warmer. And there was an ice-cream store across the street where she could probably buy a strawberry shake.

When she was growing up, a strawberry shake had been her treat every year for her birthday. Her parents had made sure of it, even if they just went to a fast-food place and not a real ice-cream parlor. She'd sworn that when she grew up, she'd have strawberry milkshakes whenever she wanted them, whether it was in the middle of the day, the middle of the morning, or the middle of the night.

After Alycia ate, she'd get a double and have it for dinner.

She smiled. Things were going to be okay. Here she'd panicked about making this trip alone, and she was doing fine. She was even confident enough to call her birth daughter's foster mom.

She crossed to her bag and dug Shana's number out of the outer pocket, then dialed the number, keeping her mind purposefully blank. A woman's voice answered on the third ring. A pleasant, feminine sound.

"Shana Devlin?"

"Yes, this is Shana."

"This is Layla Marino."

"Layla, hello!" Shana greeted her as though she were an old friend she'd been worrying about but hadn't had time to call. "Did you arrive safely? Are you in Seattle?"

"Yes. At a hotel in Pioneer Square." She gave Shana the name and address.

"Wonderful! You're not far from Keith's town house at all. You found everything okay? How did the baby survive the trip—or should I be asking how *you* survived it?"

"Fine. We're both fine." She grimaced at how her own halting words contrasted with Shana's effortless chatter.

"Good. Brett's told me a little about you and I am really looking forward to meeting you, Layla. You sound like an amazing woman."

"Thank you." She clenched her jaw. *Damn it, Layla, say something else.* "He said nice things about you, too."

"Well, there's a first." She tossed off the line as if it was habit.

Layla frowned. "I think he really means them."

"I know." Shana's voice grew gentle as if she was talking to an idiot child. "I was kidding."

Layla felt her face grow hot. Damn. She couldn't do this, couldn't manage around strangers at all. "Sorry. I should have known."

"Nonsense. You've never met me. For all you know I could be an ungrateful neurotic mess of a sister. It was a natural mistake. You'll get used to the way we tease each other in time."

"Okay." Layla clenched the receiver, totally out of her depth. What did she mean, Layla would get used to it? How exactly did she think that would happen?

The line went silent and Layla had a feeling there was a lot more Shana wanted to say on this subject but was keeping it to herself.

"So, Bruce Lehr, Alycia's uncle..."

"Yes?" Layla held her breath. The man who wanted to adopt Alycia.

"He's been anxious for your arrival. He wants to talk to you—not about anything intense, just to say hi and smooth the way."

"I see." Nothing intense? What could they possibly say to each other that wouldn't be intense, even if they were discussing the weather?

"He asked me to give you his number. Do you think you could call him tonight and let him know you arrived? I'll do it if you don't want to, but I know he'd love to hear from you."

"No, I'll call." She wrote the number down with a shaky hand. Right now she'd love Shana to make the call, but she wasn't a coward, and she was getting much too close to acting like one. "I'll call him right away."

"Thanks." Shana cleared her throat. Layla tensed

instinctively, as if she wasn't quite tense enough to begin with. "I know this is hard for you, Layla, for everyone, but—"

"Yes." Layla cut her off. Rude, she knew, but she didn't want to hear that she was brave, or that she was doing the right thing, or that both children deserved to be with their blood relations, or all three. Didn't want to hear any of it. "I'm sorry. It's just that…"

"I understand." Shana's response was quick, warm and sincere.

Layla's throat thickened. "Thanks."

"So you have the directions here? You'll come by and see us in the morning? To meet Phoebe?"

"I…yes." She squeezed her eyes shut. "I'll be there."

"Around nine?"

"Sounds good."

"Okay, then. We'll see you at—"

"Shana?" Layla opened her eyes and stared at her pale, tight features in the room's wall mirror.

"Yes?"

Dozens of words and phrases swept through Layla's head. What could she say? "Thanks. You've been very nice. To me and…Phoebe."

"You're welcome." A smile sounded in Shana's voice. "She's a lovely child—you should be proud of her."

"Yes." Layla said goodbye, hung up the phone and stood rigidly, fists clenched at her sides. She was fine. This was all fine.

She stared at the number scrawled on the notepad, not remotely wanting to invite more emotional up-heaval. *Just do it, Layla.*

The more she thought about it, the more calling the

Lehrs would seem like an insurmountable task, and the more she'd want to put Baby back in the car and drive home, stick her head in the sand and ignore the world as she'd been doing for the past eight years. She couldn't do that anymore. The late Jim and Patty Lehr had made sure of that the minute they'd taken Phoebe away from her.

Layla dialed, her palm sweating against the cold plastic of the receiver next to her ear.

"Hello?" The male voice was rich, deep, confident. From the distortion on the line, Layla guessed she'd reached Bruce Lehr's cell phone.

"This is Layla Marino." She could barely get the words out.

"Who?" He raised his voice over the static on the line.

"Layla Marino. I've got your niece." She fought the absurd urge to giggle. She sounded like a kidnapper about to demand ransom.

"Layla! Hang on."

She heard him mumble words to someone and an excited female response. He'd greeted her the same way Shana had, like someone he already knew and liked, someone he'd been hoping to hear from.

"Layla?" The static disappeared from the line; his voice was clear and strong. "That better? I pulled over. It's hell to hear when the car is moving."

"Yes. I can hear you."

"Good. So the trip was okay? You arrived okay?"

"Yes." She glanced at Alycia, who was starting to get restless in her seat. "We're both fine."

"I'm glad. Anne, my wife, and I...that is...we're so grateful to you for what you've done for her. After what my brother must have put you through..."

"Oh. Well..." She made an impatient movement. She was utterly at a loss with all these smooth, cheery people. "She's a wonderful girl."

"I'm sure." His voice dropped to low and husky. "We have a lot to offer her. We already love her very much."

"Yes." Layla's throat clamped tight; her chest swelled. He sounded sincere, a nice man. Alycia would be better off with them. They were well off, Brett had told her. Educated, well-traveled, madly in love—ideal candidates for adoption. Alycia would have every advantage, a stable two-parent home, playmates all around.

"You must be exhausted after your drive. I won't keep you. But thanks, Layla. Your call means the world to us. We look forward to meeting you soon."

"Me, too. Thank you." She hung up the phone, her body starting to shake from tension. Alycia let out her excuse-me-but-I'm-hungry wail, and Layla picked her up, crossed to the maroon velour armchair and sank into it, struggling to find a comfortable position to nurse.

Alycia latched on and began sucking vigorously. Layla allowed herself to look down, smooth the soft hair, experience the warmth of the little body that fit hers so well—and felt a stab of horrible pain.

Immediately she looked away and focused on the dreadful painting on the wall of a tiny white house so surrounded by flowers it looked as if it was being choked. On the porch sat a little girl holding a bright red poppy.

Layla focused on the girl, forcing her breathing to calm. She was doing fine, remember?

A loud knock came at the door. Layla jumped. Baby startled and started wailing. Damn, the crib.

Layla stood, heart still thumping, and hurriedly pulled down her shirt. She went to answer, bringing the screaming bundle awkwardly with her, feeling as though she was being invaded.

A sullen boy wheeled in the collapsed crib and went about setting it up.

The room was starting to get hot from the overactive heater. A man lunged out into the hall and shouted at his friend; their door slammed.

Baby continued to scream for her interrupted dinner. Layla put her on her shoulder and shushed her gently, patting the indignant back. Was this guy going to take forever?

She closed her eyes and thought about what she most wanted. Her cabin, her peace, her mountain.

And Brett.

She tried to turn off the thought, tried to push him away as she'd managed to do all day, but this time it didn't work. Her heart squeezed, her lungs squeezed, the heat and the screaming baby squeezed her until she was ready to shout, to hand the child to the sullen boy and to run screaming out into the cold, gray city.

Watching Brett leave her, watching him get in his car and drive away, had been the closest she could imagine to what it must feel like to be dying. Letting him go was the right decision. Staying with him, growing more and more dependent on him could only make the pain worse later.

She knew it was right. Her heart told her, her brain told her. But, God, she wanted him here with her right now. His strength, his comfort, his humor…

He'd kissed her this morning, or tried to before

she'd cut it short to avoid the agony. He'd even lowered his considerable pride to ask again if he could
come with her.

She'd refused, her insides hammering at her to let
him, let him, *let him.* Then she'd watched his face shut
down and heard those horrible impersonal words,
"Okay, goodbye then." And watched him drive away.
Back to Nebraska, back to the rest of his life. He'd
undoubtedly meet someone else. Marry someday.
Think of her fondly as the girl he once knew. It was
intolerable.

"Okay, all set, ma'am." The Sullen One gave miserable Baby a dirty look as if it was somehow the
child's fault that he'd interrupted her dinner and comfort.

He left, the door slamming behind him. Layla ran
to lower the heat, collapsed into the chair and guided
Baby's head back onto her breast.

Baby. She'd slipped into calling her that all over
again.

The crying stopped, the sucking resumed, interrupted once in a while by a shuddering hiccup as Baby
wound down from her adventures in screaming. Layla
hugged her close, then when the pain was too much,
she eyed the little girl on the porch in the picture
again, wondered if she had a mom inside the house
baking cookies that smelled wonderful, a dad who
would come home and scoop her in his arms and act
as if the gift of the red poppy was the most amazing
thing he'd ever been given.

She bent her head again to look at the child nursing
at her breast.

Alycia. Her name was Alycia. And she deserved to

have that life with Bruce and Anne. The life she was meant to have.

Layla would get her birth child back and raise Phoebe alone in a cabin. Her child would grow up with a weird, cold mother, a gun named Jake, a father she'd never know, and another man who'd made it through to her mother's cold heart. Who, even though he had left this morning, would never ever go away.

CHAPTER TWELVE

BRETT RANG THE DOORBELL at Keith's town house and braced himself for the astonishment and immediate slide into speculation he knew his presence on Shana's doorstep would spark.

He'd driven down Layla's mountain yesterday and turned west toward Seattle without the slightest hesitation. She needed him, she was just too damn proud or stubborn or whatever the hell she was to admit it. And he was damned if he was going to let her go through this ordeal by herself. She could spout that "I'm fine—I love being alone" stuff until she turned green, but her eyes and her body had all been yelling "Wait. Don't leave. I need you."

He'd see her through this process whether she ever admitted that she needed him or not. Then he'd leave her to her baby and her mountain—he had no illusions there was forever in their cards—but not until he was sure she was going to be okay.

The door opened. He grinned at his sister. Here it came. *Brett!*

"Brett!"

What are you doing here?

"What are you doing here?"

He chuckled and grabbed her in a bear hug. It had been entirely too long since he'd laid eyes on her. He held her away from him, unable to stop grinning.

"You look fabulous." He squinted, studying her. "Something's different. Your hair?"

He knew it wasn't that. Her auburn hair was in the same style she'd had it in for years.

"No." She looked at him curiously, as if she couldn't imagine what he was talking about.

He shrugged and released her, unable to identify what it was, sure it was something. "Maybe you just look a ton older."

"Oh, thanks a *lot*." She punched him playfully on the shoulder. "Come in. Come in. I'm dying for you to meet Keith. And...the baby."

His heart gave a jab of painful excitement. Phoebe. Layla's birth daughter.

"Then I want to know exactly what lured you out of retirement to pay a visit." She lifted one eyebrow and gave him a comically speculative look. "Though I can guess."

"Oh?" He didn't want to touch that one.

"I'm thinking her name is—"

"Brett!" A tall, handsome man came into the stylish living room, hand extended, warm smile on his face. "Nice to meet you."

Brett shook his hand, sizing him up, and was pleased to find he instinctively liked the man. Not that he would have caused Shana a moment's grief if he didn't. "Sorry to drop in on you unannounced."

"Nonsense." Keith put his arm around Shana and they exchanged a gooey glance. "You're family. Always welcome."

"Thanks." Brett glanced around the room to hide his unease. He couldn't say he'd have been that gracious if the situation had been reversed. When Alexandra, his stepsister, had shown up in Nebraska to invite her to his wedding, he'd all but thrown her out, not that he'd ever have treated Shana's boyfriend that way.

At the time he'd felt entirely justified telling her to butt out of his life. Now, with a new perspective he couldn't quite understand, he was starting to think he'd been a stupendous, Class-A jerk. Maybe he should visit Alexandra while he was here in town. Apologize and put things right, even if he didn't end up going to the wedding.

"Where is Phoebe?" He was half eager, half nervous to see the child. Would she look like Layla? Like her father?

"Phoebe's napping." Shana glanced at her watch. "Four-thirty. She should be up soon, though. Layla's coming to see her tomorrow morning at nine."

They both watched him carefully—both pretending they weren't—to gauge his reaction. He tried for a casual interest, but emotion gripped his throat. She was here. She'd made it. God, she was brave.

"She called?"

"Yes." Shana wasn't even pretending not to stare now. "Shortly after she got in."

He moved restlessly, wanting to know everything. How had she sounded? Was she all right? Had the drive been stressful? Was Alycia handling the new surroundings okay?

"Terrif—" He cleared his throat. "Terrific."

Shana and Keith immediately became tremendously busy.

"I'm on my way to Krueger's to get takeout for dinner and some of their fabulous coffee cake for tomorrow morning when Layla comes." Keith exchanged glances with Shana, then turned to Brett. "Anything you feel like particularly, Brett?"

"I'll eat anything."

"You know about Layla?"

He nodded. Multigrain porridge with apricots and raisins for breakfast. Peanut-butter sandwiches, chunky one side, smooth on the other, jelly in between, cut diagonally into quarters for lunch.

"I think she likes everything, too."

"Good enough." Keith kissed Shana and shot her another meaningful glance before he left the room.

Brett made himself smile at his sister. No sense letting on how involved he'd gotten in the baby issue. Why give her more fuel for her you're-a-softy-inside tirades?

He'd done a lot of thinking on his way down Layla's mountain. Away from her it was easier to think clearly. No question he'd fallen harder in a couple of days than he ever would have thought possible. But what he had to keep in mind was that he was only talking about a couple of days. He couldn't make any kind of long-term judgment after a blink of time like that. Especially given the extraordinary circumstances of their short acquaintance.

Not to mention the fact that his and Layla's long-term goals were decidedly different. He was always on the go; he wouldn't make any kind of decent boyfriend, let alone anything more permanent, if that's where this led. Every woman he'd ever been involved with had gotten frustrated by his lack of…presence in the relationship.

With Layla it might be different—he couldn't exactly see her being clingy. But with Layla there was also the small problem that she wanted to live on top of a mountain entirely by herself. Which put a decided damper on intimacy. And he'd be damned if he'd cut himself off from humanity to be close to her. Nothing between them, however strong it might turn out to be, could survive those confined quarters.

He didn't think it was a healthy way for her kid to grow up either. A big part of his growing up had been the other kids in his neighborhood. Granted, they'd also been the cause of a lot of his undoing, but for the most part, good things had come out of those friendships.

Layla's daughter would grow up to be pretty odd. Too mature, too serious, socially awkward. Layla needed to get off that mountain, get to someplace where she—

He shook himself out of that train of thought. Layla wasn't his responsibility. He'd grown to care for her, and had preceded her here to make sure she survived the transition with as little pain as possible. Then they'd go their separate ways. What was best for her and her daughter was up to her to figure out.

"Hello? Anyone home?"

He brought his hand down from its pensive stroking of his jaw and gave Shana a sheepish smile. "Yeah, I'm here."

"Dubious."

She winked at him and he rolled his eyes. The woman knew him entirely too well.

"Would you like to see Phoebe now?"

"I thought she was asleep."

"She just announced she's awake." Shana smiled mischievously and batted her eyes in feigned surprise. "Rather loudly. You didn't hear?"

The baby noises were obvious now that he tuned

in. What had he said about Layla clouding up his brain on that mountain? "I hear her."

Shana gave him that I-know-what's-up look of hers that used to make him nuts when she was a smug teenager whose older brother had gotten in trouble once again. This time he shrugged and grinned, which made her laugh out loud.

The sight clicked his vague sense that she'd changed somehow into sharp focus.

"I know what's different about you." He followed her through a back hallway to the room where the baby must sleep. "You're happy."

She stopped outside the closed door and turned back with a smile that practically made her glow. He had an instant desire to see that smile, that kind of inner light, on Layla. See how she looked without the control and without the shadows.

"I'm beyond happy, Brett." She held up her left hand, on which a generous diamond solitaire sparkled. Of course he hadn't noticed it to save his life—what was with him?

"Keith asked me to marry him last week. I was waiting until you got back to Nebraska to call, but telling you in person is even better."

"Wow." He laughed in sheer amazement at the concept of his little sister getting married. Not that it was a total surprise—he knew Keith was someone really special in her life. But *wow* was about the size of it.

He gathered her close, probably squeezing the life out of her. Emotion tightened his chest. He was so damn happy for her. And maybe a little envious.

"No wonder you were glowing like neon. I'm thrilled for you, tadpole."

He pulled back and grinned when she didn't even grimace at the hated nickname. This was good for her; he felt it in his bones.

"Being in love with someone really right for you is the best feeling in the world." She wiped away a tear and narrowed her eyes teasingly above a smile that wouldn't quit. "And unless I am wrong, I think you are headed toward finding that out."

This time he didn't bother to pretend. "I'm not right for her. No one is. Our lives are utterly different. And the woman has a force field around her heart and her property and her life that not even Faucet Man could penetrate."

She laughed at the reference to their favorite invented superhero. "Ah, but Faucet Man had only a Super Immortal Wrench and the Power Blaster Spigot of Truth. You've got a lot more appropriate weapons for the job."

"It isn't in the cards, Shana."

"We'll see. I have a feeling—"

An insistent baby wail came through the door and saved him from whatever she was about to say. Shana smirked at what was probably a look of half panic on his face, and opened the door slowly. She peeked her head in and grinned. "Look who's here! Look who's awake!"

A long, drawn-out, *Aaaaaaa,* emerged through the doorway and wrapped itself around Brett's heart. He moved into the room, nervous as hell, as if he was going to meet someone in a position of tremendous power over his future.

Two feet from the low, portable crib, he stopped, feeling as if someone had collapsed both his lungs.

There was no question that this was Layla's child.

The straight sharp nose might not have evolved yet, but the eyes were pure Layla. Beautifully shaped and full of light and intelligence, minus the serious guarded look. The mouth was hers, too, generous and curving. The thin gold hair wanted to curl, not hang straight—maybe her father had given her that. But whatever cynical feelings Brett had about love at first sight for women, there was no question he could feel it for a baby. For this baby.

He reached his arms over the sides, sending Shana a questioning glance. She nodded, beaming and looking even more smug. He didn't care.

He picked the child up, cradling her head, and held her, inhaling the sweet baby scent of her hair before he settled her away from him and smiled at her.

She gave him a wary frown.

"Uh-oh." He grinned at her.

Phoebe frowned harder.

"You're not going to shoot at me like your mom did, are you?"

The little face opened in surprise, then split into the hugest grin he'd ever seen. Her tiny frame heaved with what he swore was the beginnings of wheezy baby laughter.

That was it. He was gone.

"Looks like someone has gotten a soft spot for babies. Never thought I'd see that."

He shrugged and made a face at Phoebe to get her to smile again. "They're not so bad when you get to know them."

Shana burst out laughing. "You think I've changed. You amaze me."

"Do I?"

He opened his mouth and eyes wide for the baby

and was rewarded with another enormous grin. He laughed and did it again just for the joy of seeing her happy. This child was Layla's little clone, no question. And every instinct he had was telling him that just seeing her birth baby, looking so unquestionably like her, would raise the cold curtain off Layla's heart.

He lifted Phoebe up, pressed a kiss to her impossibly smooth forehead and admitted to himself what he'd spent far too much time denying.

When that curtain came up, he wanted in, too.

BABY—ALYCIA—STARTED TO WAIL. Layla sat up in the strange, too soft bed, already awake, and pushed off the thin, clammy, vaguely sticky blanket, which was made of some material that wasn't found anywhere in nature, she was certain. She wasn't sure she'd slept for more than an hour or two all night. Noises in the hall, noises out on the street—how did people sleep in all this chaos? Her head hurt; her eyes were dry. How had she survived all those years sleeping with two or three families in the same tiny one-bedroom trailer or rental?

Just a question of what you were used to. Well, she was damn sure glad she was used to privacy and space and peace now.

She picked Alycia up out of her crib. The child hadn't slept well, either, waking every two hours or so, wanting food or comfort. Layla couldn't blame her. The hotel atmosphere was as strange and disconcerting to the baby as it was to her.

Of course, a lot of Layla's trouble sleeping hadn't been because of the noise. She had to go to Keith and Shana's town house today. Meet Brett's younger sister. Be polite and chatty, while keeping her emotions locked in an iron safe.

She kissed Alycia's soft hair, though she was the one who needed comfort. Shana's and Bruce's friendliness on the phone had been all about manners they were brought up with. These people didn't really care about her. She was an oddity to them, a freak, a woman whose own child was stolen from her and she hadn't even noticed. A woman who lived away from people. Never mind that she'd sold her pottery creations to CEOs and movie stars and interior designers from L.A. to Seattle. Never mind she could chop wood, build, shoot, make her own way all by herself.

To them she'd be poor Layla, migrant worker's daughter, probably some kind of half-wit product of in-breeding.

For the first time since Brett told her yesterday morning how the switch actually happened, anger spurted through her at Patty and Jim Lehr, the couple who had done this horrible thing on purpose. How dare they steal her child because they thought their own infant might be ill and die as their first daughter had? How dare they toss away their own flesh and blood as if she was a blemished piece of fruit? Didn't an ill child deserve love and support from her own mother the same as any healthy child? Probably twice as much, if her time on this earth was to be short.

And why the hell hadn't they just checked with the nurse to see if their new daughter had the same form of Downs that had killed their first? Granted, Alycia had a rough trip through the birth canal, as Layla's birth daughter had, but she was healthy as a horse. Most babies didn't look quite right after delivery. Even

Layla knew that, and she'd only had one, and nothing but a book and occasional clinic visits for information.

This woman had given her child away when there was every hope the baby would be fine. She'd done it, thinking Layla would have to care for a sick child for a few months before the baby passed away and left her grief-stricken for the rest of her life, while they could raise Layla's healthy daughter themselves.

It was a damn good thing Alycia's mother and father had died in the car crash, or Layla would be tempted to help them in that direction herself.

She took a deep, calming breath, which didn't do much calming but did stop her thoughts from going down that particularly pointless path any further. Yes, she was angry; she had every right to be angry. Hell, she had every right to every homicidal thought she could conjure up. But she also had to recognize that her own fears were being channeled to make the anger worse. She couldn't blame the Lehrs, however ignorant and misguided their actions were, for her own fear and failure as a mother. Or for her own decision to travel north to Glacier in the last week of her pregnancy. To have the baby as far away from Leavenworth and people who knew her as she could get.

She only needed to drive to Shana and Keith's house, be polite, see the baby, find out what she had to do to make the switch, and get out, back here, to this relatively safe place. She could do it. She could do it fine. What came after that, the weeks of legal issues and police files and paperwork, she would worry about later.

Right now she just needed to get through today.

Alycia finished nursing. Layla put her to her shoulder to burp her, and looked at the gold watch her grandmother left her, focusing her tired eyes on her unsteady wrist. She should have breakfast.

The thought of eating in a restaurant under strangers' eyes made her stomach churn more. She wasn't even wild about the idea of someone barging into her room again with a tray. But she couldn't starve.

She got up from the maroon velour chair, ridiculously close to tears, and picked up a room service menu, balancing Alycia on her other arm. Eggs, pancakes, bacon, sausage, French toast—damn it, didn't anyone eat oatmeal?

Tears rose in her eyes; she was desperately out of her element, even in the relatively safe anonymity of a hotel room. She couldn't even have what she wanted to eat.

A heavy knock sounded at the door. Layla jumped and gave a muffled cry, which set Alycia off. Damn. *Damn.* What was with these people? Hadn't she put out the Do Not Disturb sign last night?

The knock came again, barely audible over Alycia's wailing. She wouldn't answer. Let them go to hell.

She rocked Alycia as soothingly as she could, given her own state of near-freakout, and got the baby's volume back down. The knock came again, this time with a male voice she could barely hear and didn't recognize. Housekeeping? This early? Why didn't they leave her alone?

Still rocking the baby and murmuring soothingly in a shaky voice, she walked toward the door and peered through the peephole.

A huge gasp sucked all her air in and wouldn't let it come back out for several long seconds.

Brett.

She fumbled with the door chain and pulled open the door. *Brett.*

"Hi." He grinned at what must be a look of utter-stupid-speechless astonishment on her face. Utter-stupid-speechless astonishment that was quickly turning to joy and relief at seeing his wonderful, handsome, familiar face in this bizarre place, in this bizarre situation.

"Hi." She backed away from the door to let him in, staring as if he might disappear at any second and prove her doubt in her ability to believe her eyes.

"How's Alycia?" He touched the child's head, resting on Layla's shoulder. Alycia lifted her face toward him and rewarded him with a smile and a belch that made her entire body lift.

"Damn glad to see me, I take it." He touched Layla's face with his warm, strong hand, brushed some hair away from her cheek. "And how's Mom?"

"I'm fine." The denial was stiff and automatic.

One brow lifted, then his forehead creased into a worried frown and he put his arms around the two of them. "That bad, huh?"

She resisted for a second, then allowed her head to rest against his solid chest. That's all it took. Her entire body started the long way it had to go toward relaxing. He was here. She could handle everything if he was here with her. If that made her weak and helpless, everything she swore to herself she'd never be, then tough. It was only for a moment. Only for as long as he was here.

"I'm glad you came." She whispered the words so softly she wasn't sure he'd heard them. Until he bent his head down and she lifted her head up and he kissed her over and over, warm kisses that turned passionate and desperate.

Alycia let out a screech of protest.

"I think we're squashing her." Her voice came out low and shaky.

He released her with a final soft kiss, took Alycia and put her in her seat.

Layla watched him, not quite able to get herself to understand that he hadn't left after all. That he wasn't in Nebraska; he was here to help her through this. She couldn't remember ever feeling so happy to see anyone in her life. His big, confident body brightened and warmed the room, dispelling the sterility and lifelessness with his mere presence, giving her strength and confidence of her own in the process.

"There, little one. You be happy for a bit. I need to talk to Layla."

Alycia's features crumpled and he held up a stern finger, then fished in his pocket. "Nope. None of that."

He produced a brightly colored soft toy that made bell sounds when it moved, and attached it to the Velcro loops on the toy bar above her seat. He gave it a push and Alycia smiled at the tinkling sound and stared, fascinated as it continued to sway.

"When did you get here?" Layla moved toward him; she couldn't help it.

"Before you did." He moved toward her as if he couldn't help it, either, so close she had to look up to see his face. "I drove down your mountain and due west."

She smiled and shook her head. "Even though I told you—"

"I *heard* what your mouth said." He put his arms

around the small of her back, pulled her to him so they were joined from the hips down, and leaned forward to kiss her again. "But I listened to the rest of you."

She wound her arms around his neck and kissed him back with her heart, allowing herself to need him, just for this little while. His arms tugged her body tight against his; he tilted her head back into the crook of his arm and kissed her more, held her powerless, until her body was begging for all of him.

"Brett."

His hand slid up the back of her shirt and made warm wonderful circles on her bare skin.

"*Brett.*"

"Mmm?" He kissed her throat, her cheek.

"Not in front of Alycia."

He gave her an incredulous look. "She's two months old. What does she know?"

"I just can't."

He grinned. "I wasn't going to ravish you in front of Alycia. We need to get going."

Layla's smile drooped. Her stomach got butterflies of an entirely different kind. "Yes."

"But—" he kissed her fiercely again "—I do intend to ravish you at some point soon."

"We can't—"

He held up a finger the way he had with Alycia. "No. None of that."

She chuckled. God, it was good to see him. All the awkwardness she'd felt talking to other people simply didn't exist with him.

He stopped grinning, a strange light in his eyes. "There's something here, Layla, between us. We can't go on pretending there isn't."

She swallowed over the lump in her throat. "One thing at a time. Okay?"

"Okay." His grin came back, a little more forced this time. "A couple of things before we go. One, I spoke to Jaron Dorsey, in charge of this investigation. He'll want to talk to you, ask a few questions, go over your story, okay?"

"Yes." She sighed. Yes. Of course. More people, more prying.

"I told him what I knew already. But one question he asked, which I didn't know the answer to, was why you'd go nearly to the Canadian border, to Glacier, to have your baby when you live in the center of the state."

Layla hunched her shoulders and bent her head to examine the rug. How the hell could she tell this confident, in-charge man that everything in her had begged her to leave town? That, like a cat who disappears from the home she was raised in to have her kittens, Layla had wanted to be away to have her child. Away from interference, conjecture, from anyone who knew her or would see her again.

She'd just gone. Spent the last week of her pregnancy on the road, stopping every few hours to walk and keep her circulation going strong. Just driving, exploring. Making sure she spent the night in towns big enough to have hospitals—she wasn't taking any foolish chances with her baby's safety. Enjoying the late summer scenery and the beginnings of fall. Taking some time to contemplate the huge changes that were about to hit her life. If only she'd known....

And then she'd hit Glacier and her contractions had started in a tiny motel on the edge of town.

"Come on, Layla." His voice was gently teasing. "You can tell me."

"I…just wanted to be away." The rug was a dull brownish color, flecked with white. Ugly. Utilitarian.

Alycia gurgled and let out a short wail, which ended when her hand accidentally hit one of her jingling toys.

Layla raised her head, unable to stand waiting for his reaction any longer. Did he think her beyond strange? Even stranger than he found her already?

To her surprise he was looking at her with tenderness—slightly bemused tenderness—and a kind of sorrow she'd never seen on his face before.

"You think I'm a nutcase."

His features rearranged themselves into a smile. "No. I just hope someday you'll run *to* people when you need them, instead of away."

Layla bit her lip. She had no idea what to say to that. Not the slightest. She wanted to slug him for his judgment of her and she wanted to kiss him for caring and she wanted to block out the fact that he might very well be telling her something important that she needed to listen to.

She made an impatient gesture. Right now she just wanted to get this day over. "I don't—"

"One thing at a time." He held his hand up to stop her. "You already said that. Never mind."

"Okay." She smiled at him. He was so good to her.

"You had breakfast yet?"

"No." She threw off the weirdness of their conversation and managed to make her smile genuine. Her worries over where to eat suddenly seemed ridiculous. "I've gotten so bad I was afraid to go eat in public."

He strode over to Alycia, hooked his arm through

the carrier handle and lifted the seat. "Our new mantra—one thing at a time. First, a drive-thru for breakfast. Then maybe a cafeteria for lunch. And when you're ready, a real, live human waitress. One you can teach about the finer points of making peanut butter and salad."

"Oh, for—" She laughed and went to put on her coat.

Her life wasn't made any less complicated by his presence—maybe more so. But the ordeal she had to go through this morning, and for God knew how long after, would now be a whole lot easier to take. Even if he could only stay a day or two.

One thing at a time. And the way she felt now, she'd bet that with Brett Devlin beside her, she could make it through just about anything.

CHAPTER THIRTEEN

BY THE TIME they arrived at Keith's house—Brett driving Layla's Cherokee, Alycia in her car seat in back—any euphoria that had seeped into Layla's mood had vanished. She felt anxious, angry, and wearier than she ever could remember feeling. The city sapped her—the crowds, the traffic, the endless over-stimulation. That feeling of being alien, of not belonging, which was so easy to dispel with Brett in the privacy of her hotel room, had crept back to erode her self-confidence.

All that would be bad enough without the reason for her visit. She'd have to go into Shana's house and face her worst fear. To see a child that belonged to her, or would soon, in every sense of the word, and feel nothing. Her own daughter would be a stranger to her. Worse, Shana and Brett would be looking on, expecting a tender mother-daughter reunion suitable for a greeting-card commercial.

She lay back against the seat, eyes closed, fists on her thighs, and felt Brett's hand cover hers. She opened her eyes to smile at him, unclenched her fingers and turned her palm up to clasp his. The load on her heart lightened a little. He was with her, at least this morning.

She couldn't look beyond today, tomorrow or however long he'd stay. Sooner or later they'd have to go their separate ways. She accepted that. But right now, his being here meant the world to her. She hoped he knew that.

"Brett."

He slowed to stop for a red light and glanced over at her, did a double take and grasped her chin to pull her forward for a quick kiss. "What, Layla-mine?"

She felt herself blush hotly at his endearment. She wouldn't be his forever, but she sure as hell was his right now. "I'm just glad you're here. And thanks for knowing what I needed."

He grinned and let go of her chin. "Heck, it was what *I* needed. I couldn't stand the thought of you going through all this by yourself. I would have gone nuts wondering how you were handling it. Purely selfish."

She chuckled and shook her head.

"What?" He feigned innocent puzzlement. "You think I care about *you?*"

"Yeah." Her chuckles died away. She made an effort to keep her voice light. "I think maybe you do."

"I think maybe you're right." The light turned green. He gassed the jeep forward. "That go both ways?"

"Yes." She barely got the word out. Why was talking about this stuff so hard?

"What?" He put his hand to his ear, like an old man trying to hear. "What was that?"

Layla giggled. He was doing his best to put her at ease, and she was about to burst from gratitude.

"Yes, I care about you," she shouted.

He glanced over at her with a wink and squeezed her hand again. "Did I tell you my sister got herself engaged last week?"

"No!" She looked down at the hand holding hers, strong and capable, and felt a strange pang of envy. "I'll be sure to congratulate her."

"She'll like that." He slowed the car. "Here we are."

They pulled up to a gorgeous row of brownstone town houses and parked on the street in front. Brett yanked the keys out of the ignition and glanced back at Alycia before returning his gaze to Layla, concern evident in his eyes.

"Ready?"

Layla nodded, convinced she never would be, so why bother telling the truth? She got out of the car into the gray, cloudy, November chill and opened the back door to take the sleeping Alycia out of her seat. She held the warm, limp bundle close to her for one delicious baby-scented moment before she put her resolutely in the carrier Brett had unloaded from the back of the car.

She felt like a traitor to this child for not fighting to keep her, for going along the route of least resistance. Even knowing that what had happened wasn't her fault. Even knowing she was doing the best thing for Alycia. Giving her the kind of life Layla could never give her, a home with two loving parents and all the advantages. Even knowing the child she was going to meet in this house in a few short minutes was truly destined to be hers.

The front door to Keith's town house opened and a tall, attractive woman with reddish hair emerged, smiling warmly and waving. A handsome, even taller man dressed in stylish casual clothes came out onto the front step and stood with her, arm around her waist. The two of them looked so content, so suburban.

Shana was lovely, dressed in tapered pants and a burgundy sweater. She looked sweet and feminine, thoroughly poised and at ease.

Layla looked down at her own clothes. All she owned were jeans and sweats. Her only coat was this old parka. She had no makeup, no hairstyle. She felt exactly the same way she had in the classroom when she'd first encountered Phoebe's namesake, nearly twenty years ago, spotless and fresh in her white dress with red cherries and little red shoes.

Her breath caught in her throat; she stopped walking. She couldn't do this. She could barely breathe.

"Have I ever told you—" Brett caught her elbow and turned her toward him, the intensity of his gaze holding hers "—how beautiful you are on cloudy horrible days when you're about to meet the child you gave birth to, who was switched away by two horrible, selfish people?"

"Brett..." She tried to pull away but he held on to her tightly.

"Second only to how beautiful you are on sunny days, which, come to think of it, I've never seen you on, but I know I'm right, *and*..." He resisted her efforts to pull away a second time, but she could feel her lips wanting to curve into a smile, and her breathing calmed.

"Have I ever told you that none of those hold a candle to how beautiful you are in the evening in the woods with the snow around you, or in the middle of the night in the firelight?"

She gave a helpless chuckle and stopped trying to pull away. "No. But thank you."

He nodded, let his fingers slip down her forearm until he reached her hand, squeezed and let go.

"I wasn't lying, so don't start saying I was just trying to make you feel better, either, okay?"

She rolled her eyes, unable to stop smiling. He had a way of making her entire world okay, no matter how badly or how fast it was crumbling.

"Come meet my sister."

She took in a deep breath and straightened her shoulders. "I'm ready."

They walked up to the smiling couple. Layla caught herself wanting to inspect their front walk and forced herself to keep looking up and smiling back. She was who she was. She owed these people no apology.

The curiosity and pity she dreaded were both there in Shana's face. But what Layla didn't expect was the warmth of the gaze. A warmth that had nothing to do with fake hospitality and everything to do with accepting Layla into her home on the arm of her brother. As if she belonged there.

"Welcome." Shana stepped forward and extended her hand. "As you probably guessed, I'm Shana, little sister and pummeling bag to big brother Brett."

"Ha!" Brett rubbed his arm along Layla's back, a warm, reassuring touch. "I think the pummeling generally goes the other way."

"It's nice to meet you." Layla shook Shana's hand, surprised when the other woman squeezed hard before she let go. "Congratulations on your engagement. Brett just told me."

"Thanks." Shana exchanged a loving glance with Keith, who stepped forward and extended his hand.

"Hello, Layla. I'm Keith Hewitt. Welcome."

"Thank you. And more congratulations to you." She met his eyes warily, but found no censure there, nothing but grave respect, warmth and welcome.

What was with these guys?

The internal joke made her smile. Had she become such a Scrooge that she'd forgotten people were capable of good?

"Come on in out of this horrible damp weather." Shana gestured Layla into the house. "Makes your hair curly, but that's about all it's good for."

Layla's smile faded. As long as she was outside, she could pretend to forget what they were here for. One step inside and her baby could be anywhere, confronting her at any turn. She might have to come face-to-face for the first time with this little person who had come out of her own body, with all these people watching for her reaction and the child's, like a public test of her worth as a mother.

She'd never felt so vulnerable in her life.

Two more steps and she stopped and hovered in the entranceway, not sure where to go, not sure where to look. Her cheeks felt flushed, her body awkward and clumsy, as if it wasn't hers. She dared a quick, apprehensive glance around. The place was elegant, decorated with exquisite masculine taste and a fine eye for art, and smelled like something delicious had been baking earlier. No baby, though an infant swing was set up in the living room.

"Phoebe's awake." Shana laid a gentle hand on Layla's shoulder from where she stood behind her. "Would you like to see her right away? I thought it might be easier on you if she wasn't lurking in the hallway here, but at the same time I don't want you to think I'm hiding her."

"Thanks. I'd...like to see her." Her voice broke. She felt that same wild rush of disorienting suffocation she had in the hotel room right before Brett had showed up.

"Okay." Shana gave her shoulder a warm squeeze and let go. "And I'm guessing you'd like to meet her alone?"

Brett moved to stand next to her and put his arm around her waist. "Want me to come with you?"

Layla shook her head, her relief overwhelming that she wouldn't have to turn this difficult emotional moment into a spectator sport. Granted, if the baby took one look at her and burst into tears, they'd all hear, anyway, but at least she'd be spared the sight of their reaction.

"No. Thanks. I'd like to be alone with her."

She felt Brett stiffen, then withdraw. He wanted her to need him. But he'd already given her what she'd needed to get here. The rest she had to do on her own.

"Okay." He pushed her hair away from her face. "I'll be here if you change your mind."

"I know." She managed to turn and meet his eyes. "Thank you."

They stood that way for a few seconds, Layla taking strength from the warmth of his gaze. Even if she never saw him again after all this, she'd never forget the way he looked right at this moment.

"I'm ready." She glanced at Alycia, not trusting herself to kiss the child as she wanted to, and followed Shana down a narrow hallway until they reached a back bedroom, probably the guest room.

"She's in here, in her portable crib, watching her mobile. I put her down when I saw the car drive up. She's usually good for five minutes or so. She's probably on her way to being restless and will love the distraction of a new face."

Layla clenched her teeth. This woman knew her daughter intimately. Layla didn't know her at all, even what she looked like.

A movement caught her eye and she saw Brett out of her peripheral vision, standing at the other end of the hall. He was there if she changed her mind.

She wouldn't. She couldn't.

She took a step forward into the room and heard a string of baby vowels, in a voice deeper than Alycia's.

Her daughter.

She took another step, then another, stomach tight, breath held, saw the mobile, heard the tinkling music.

Then she saw her baby, and the breath came out in a long, gasping sigh. "Oh."

She moved to the low railing, gripped it until her fingers hurt. *"Oh."*

The child heard her and turned her head to investigate the noise. Mother's and daughter's eyes caught each other.

And daughter frowned.

"Phoebe." Layla reached down to touch the little yellow flannel dress, the tiny hands, the face that looked enough like the few baby pictures she'd seen of herself to be spooky. "Hello."

A bigger frown. A scowl.

Layla's breath wouldn't come out quite right. She was pretty sure her heart was using a rhythm it had never tried before.

"Hello, sweetheart," she whispered.

The face was so familiar. Even more than that, it mirrored her own. Had she seen her baby in the hospital? Or just in her dreams? How could she know this child so well?

"Hi, Phoebe."

She couldn't stop touching. Tiny touches, to make sure the child was real.

"Aaaaaaa." The baby face was solemn; Phoebe moved her hand spastically toward Layla as if she were trying to touch her.

Layla picked her up, feeling flushed and hot and not at all herself. "Hello, little one."

The chubby fist moved again, and this time slugged her on the nose with a force she hadn't expected.

"Ow."

She was more startled than hurt, but the exclamation escaped her anyway.

Phoebe stared for a second, then her little face split into a huge grin, her body heaved with silent laughter.

Layla sucked in a breath so deep and long that it seemed to go on forever. At its peak, when she couldn't take in another molecule of air, she started to cry. Huge sobs that made her turn her face away so as not to startle the child. She felt a fist latch onto her hair and tug.

"Aaaaaaaa."

She cried harder. She couldn't stop. A huge rushing flood of emotion shattering the barrier she'd constructed so carefully so many years ago.

"Brett." She managed to call out his name between sobs. *"Brett."*

He was through the door in two seconds, took in the scene and moved forward to clasp both mother and daughter in his arms. As if he'd never let either one of them go.

CHAPTER FOURTEEN

LAYLA SAT IN THE HOTEL room's plush chair, Alycia cradled on her lap, feeling the long day's tension slowly start to drain away. Coming back here, to this dark, empty, silent institutional room had been heavenly. Granted, it hadn't been a remotely average day, but as the hours had dragged on at Shana's house, later and later, she'd remembered more and more why she'd chosen to escape people.

Simply put, they exhausted her.

Even wonderful, friendly people like Shana and Keith, like Bruce and Anne Lehr, who'd stopped by briefly to meet their soon-to-be-adopted daughter. Even without any of the expected judgment or cold scrutiny, even though they were all being respectful and supportive and easily talkative, they wore her out. Made her ache for a quiet moment like this one, to the point where she found it hard to be polite. How on earth did they manage to spend so much energy on chatter without needing to nap?

Maybe chatter was their way of handling the awkwardness of the day, which had been considerable. At one point, right after lunch, with Shana looking on as Layla coddled Phoebe, the baby Shana had nurtured for so long, and Layla looking on as Bruce coddled Alycia, the baby Layla had nurtured for so long, the strain had been so bizarre that Layla had burst

out laughing, a stress reaction that immediately morti-
fied her.

What would the weird cabin girl do next?

To her surprise, when she'd stammered out an ex-
planation to the expectant room, she'd gotten nothing
but chuckles and nods in response. Anne had come up
to her later and thanked her, saying she was at the
point of throwing a complete head-banging fit for the
same reason, and was grateful Layla had saved her by
bringing what they were all feeling out into the open.

That simple gesture had done a lot to heal Layla's
inner wounds and to make her feel she wasn't neces-
sarily a glowing neon Does Not Belong sign.

But she was still glad to be back here by herself.

Alycia yawned, moving her arms randomly, then
bunched up her little legs and shot them out straight.
Layla grinned and touched the soft cheek, feeling the
by-now familiar stab of pain at any tender interaction
with her baby.

She closed her eyes wearily. Not her baby.

She'd get it right someday. Phoebe was her baby.
The child who had greeted her birth mother with a
frown and a punch in the nose.

A smile crept onto Layla's face. She couldn't help
being proud of her, this child she barely knew but
recognized immediately. Couldn't help exclaiming
later on, after lunch, when the chubby little fingers
reached for a rattle Layla dangled over her face—a
feat Alycia couldn't yet accomplish. Layla hadn't even
minded Brett's teasing expression when she'd whispered this amazing fact to him, as if the child had just
recited *The Odyssey* in ancient Greek.

So, she had been captured by the little girl, her

daughter. Couldn't wait to see her again, just to make sure she was real. This was a good thing.

Alycia let out a shriek, then adopted a tremendously-pleased-with-herself expression that made Layla laugh.

"I'll miss you terribly, little one. I wish I could keep you both."

Her voice dropped off into a husky whisper. Giving up this child would be beyond horrible, even though Bruce and Anne had been everything she'd wanted for this little girl who'd turned out not to be her own flesh and blood. They were warm, approachable, loving with each other, respectful of Layla's prior claim to the child, but obviously eager to welcome Alycia into their lives. They lived in Madison Park, which Shana later told Layla was an affluent neighborhood, lots of families, excellent schools, everything a child should have.

In addition, Bruce was well tied to the legal community in town, not only through his own efforts, but because his father had been District Attorney. Though Arthur Lehr had been dead many years, his name was still well-respected. His son Bruce was confident he could get some cronies of his father's to step in to make sure the switch-back of the babies happened with all possible speed, given the complexity of the situation. He'd also taken pains to make sure the story of the mystery baby's return stayed out of the press as long as humanly possible.

Certainly not the attention Layla was used to getting from the authorities. If she'd been trying to get this mess cleared up by herself, she'd probably have to wait until Alycia and Phoebe were in college together.

But at least she was reassured now that Alycia

would be loved and well cared for. And the Lehrs had issued an open invitation to visit anytime, as Alycia's Auntie Layla.

It was for the best. She had to keep telling herself that, or she'd go nuts.

She took a deep breath, kissed Alycia fiercely and let her relax, then let her own head drop to one side, enjoying the quiet, extremely thankful the day was over. Or at least the hard part.

Brett would show up to "tuck Layla in" soon, as he promised, after visiting his stepsister Alexandra. Layla's heart gave a pang of longing. Okay, so "people" in general exhausted her, but not Brett. He'd been so magnificent today, giving her space when she needed it, tactfully herding people away from her when she'd wanted another quiet moment with her birth daughter, continuing that incredible insight he seemed to have into her thoughts and feelings and needs. Helping her navigate this alien terrain without smothering or pushing or making her feel he thought her helpless.

It had struck her forcefully how in his element he was here, among his family, among people. Taking charge came naturally to him. Maybe he thought of himself as a loner, but he wasn't one nearly to the degree she was.

He needed people. She didn't want them.

And that's how it would end with them. She'd flee gratefully back to her mountain, where she belonged, leaving two pieces of her heart behind her. One with Alycia and the other with Brett.

Her gaze drifted to the door as if staring at it would bring him here faster. Someone was vacuuming the hall—the irregular thrusting whine of the motor and the occasional bump against baseboards sounded louder as the machine approached.

She would survive. She would learn to love her natural daughter and survive as she'd survived so far, as she'd survived today. More than survived. She'd proven many important things to herself. She wasn't meant to live with people. And she wasn't crazy for thinking Alycia hadn't looked familiar in the hospital.

Jaron Dorsey had come by Shana's on his way home before dinner and stayed for a beer. Not her usual experience of police officers, but a warm, handsome, compassionate man with piercing blue eyes. He'd been forthcoming with a few more details of the case to set Layla's mind at ease.

He'd spoken to the nurse who'd been with Layla for Phoebe's delivery in the ER. Apparently Layla had actually lain with her minutes-old daughter, but only for a brief moment, while she was in and out of consciousness before the surgery.

That explained the vividness of the dreams she remembered of her child, and why Alycia looked so different than she'd expected when the nurse had handed the squalling infant to her. *I'm sorry, this isn't her.*

If she'd hadn't hemorrhaged, if she'd been clearheaded when she'd held her daughter, she could have said those words and meant them, and this entire scenario never would have happened...

And she never would have met Brett.

She stroked Alycia's hair and frowned. Would that have been better or worse? Better to have claimed her natural daughter from the start? She'd be living peacefully still, on top of her mountain. Who's to say whether she would or wouldn't have bonded deeply with her natural daughter right off the bat, as she hadn't with Alycia. Maybe she was a slow bonder. Time would tell.

But the most important thing she'd learned, the most important thing she'd proven to herself today when she'd held her beautiful daughter, sobbing, when Brett had come in and put his arms around both of them, was that her worst fear had not been realized. She no longer needed to worry that she wasn't capable of deep love.

Because, God help her, she was deeply, madly, irrevocably in love.

With Brett.

BRETT WALKED DOWN the long corridor of Layla's hotel toward Room 109, heart warming at the thought of seeing her. How long had they been apart? All of two hours? He had it bad. When he'd been involved with other women, he was always glad to see them, but rarely missed them when they were apart. Nothing like the deep, distracting hunger he'd experienced during the pleasant and necessary amends-making visit to Alexandra at her day care.

Not just selfish hunger, either, but concern. Was Layla doing okay? Was she lonely? Was Alycia reacting calmly to the unaccustomed day of people all around, or was she giving Layla trouble when Layla most needed to rest?

For crying out loud, he was turning into an old mother hen.

He'd always assumed he was a fairly arrogant, self-absorbed person, putting number one first, not allowing himself to be distracted from what he wanted to accomplish. Certainly not allowing women to distract him from what he wanted to accomplish. Now, in a matter of mere days, he'd found himself more than distracted. Layla had become number one. Her happiness concerned him more than his own. Her pleasure was more important than his.

He grinned and knocked on the hotel door, impatient to see her, touch her, hear her voice, see her smile. For Layla, he'd even turn mother hen.

The chain rattled behind the door and it swung open. Layla stood there, beaming at him.

"Hi."

Her voice was breathless, her eyes bright. His heart nearly burst out of his chest.

He moved forward, caught her around the waist with one arm, shoved the door shut behind him and walked her backward into the room until her knees hit the side of the bed and he tumbled her down on it beneath him, grinning at her helpless laughter.

"Brett, you mad, impetuous fool."

He stifled a grin at her Southern Belle impression, gave her his best I-show-no-mercy look and lowered his head to kiss her, as he'd been dying to do all day. All yesterday. Every minute since they'd woken up together in her cabin what felt like five or six years ago.

God, she tasted good; she felt good. And she was kissing him as though she damn well meant it.

They could work something out. They had to be able to work something out. But what, he hadn't a clue.

"Alycia okay?" He could pick up his head to look for himself, but he couldn't take his eyes off Ms. Layla Marino.

"Asleep."

"Mmm. Could be handy."

She chuckled and flushed sweetly. At the same time he noticed her nostrils flare and felt the faint push of her hips up against him, almost as if she couldn't help herself. The combination of passion and innocence in this woman drove him wild.

"Did you miss me?"

She lifted a brow. "It's been two hours."

"So?" He kissed her again. "Did you miss me?"

A slow smile spread over her face; she rolled her eyes and flushed even pinker. "Yes."

"Ha!" He grinned, triumph spreading through his chest. She laughed and tried to push him away, but not, he noticed, very hard. He knew what strength those arms were capable of.

"So, did you miss *me?*"

"Like mad." He caught her chin in his hand and held her gaze steady, his grin fading. "Like mad, Layla."

She opened her mouth to say something, or to laugh, or to make fun of him, he didn't know which, but he wasn't going to give her the chance to do any of them.

He kissed her and she responded passionately, wrapping her arms around his neck to pull him tightly against her. He lost himself kissing this woman—that was the only way he could describe it. He lost himself in the taste of her, in the feel of her, in the welling of emotion that made his consciousness of the rest of the room, the rest of the world, the rest of his life, fade away in relative unimportance.

He moved to unbutton her thick, soft, cotton shirt, searching her eyes for signs that she wanted him to stop.

He found none. She watched him quietly, breathing

high, color high, eyes shining with anticipation. He pulled open her shirt, dragging his hand down between her breasts, back up, back down, until the temptation was too great and he stroked her full softness, tracing the nipples with his thumb.

"You are so beautiful. Your body is so beautiful."

She looked away, writhed self-consciously. She hated when he complimented her, but she was damn well going to have to get used to it.

He kissed between her breasts, then moved down lower, opened her jeans to make way for his mouth and teased her with his tongue, loving the soft folds, loving her reaction. He could taste her this way for hours, make her climax three or four times.

But today was about the joining of their bodies, not efficient routes to orgasm. Today was about showing Layla how much he was coming to love her, how much he hoped to have her in his life.

He shed his clothes, her hands helping, stroking, driving him wild when her palm closed over his erection. He felt himself harden further, felt the burn of urgency to be inside her.

Her jeans slipped down quickly; she kicked them off with impatience that mirrored his. He put on a condom, then lay on top of her without going in just yet, savoring the feel of their naked bodies together, the soft warmth of hers fitting him just right.

He kissed her, whispered her name, kissed her again, and reached down to part her for his entry.

She was heaven. He slid home and felt the same overwhelming charge of emotion he had two nights ago in her cabin. He moved slowly, wanting their joining to go on forever, wanting just to be inside her like this, to move inside her, stroke inside her and make her feel everything he was feeling.

She wanted it faster. He could tell by the way she bucked against him, by the way she gripped his back, but this wasn't about fast, this wasn't about getting to completion. This was about what they were feeling along the way.

I love you. He felt the words so deeply he was sure she heard them. She might have, given the way she took in a sudden breath, wrapped her arms tight around his shoulders, pressed her cheek to his and met him stroke for stroke, each one a declaration of his love, an appreciation of this new world she'd brought him to.

He wasn't sure how much time had passed, maybe minutes, maybe hours, but suddenly and unexpectedly, she lifted her head, whispered in his ear what his thrusting was doing to her, and his body betrayed him.

With a groan, he pushed hard, felt her respond, felt her strain to reach her climax, harder, higher, then she cried out at the same moment the wave hit him, consumed him, then receded while he pulsed out his release.

He lay there, on her breast, listening to her breathing, feeling her heart pounding underneath his cheek.

"I could stay here forever." Of course it wasn't true, not literally, but he felt it right at that moment as if it was. "Right here, listening to you breathe."

Layla laughed softly. "I think you might get restless eventually."

"Nope." He rubbed his cheek against her soft skin. "This is it. I'm not moving. For the rest of my life."

She laughed again, but uncertainly, as if she heard

the truth behind the nonsense. He didn't want to know it frightened her. He wanted to go on thinking it was just a matter of his asking and she'd say yes.

"That was really nice."

Nice. He got a slight uneasy feeling in his stomach.

"It was amazing, Layla."

"Yes." She nodded too quickly. "It was."

The uneasy feeling became distinctly worse. He pulled out of her, kissed her tenderly and went to the bathroom to dispose of the condom. What was up with her? Was he pushing too hard, too soon?

He rubbed his forehead, eyes squeezed shut. Of course he was. The woman had gone through more today than most people went through in a lifetime. She wasn't in any shape to commit to anything more than a good night's sleep.

What had he been saying about putting her first? *Back off, Brett. Give her some room to adjust.*

He put himself into lighten-up mode and went back into the room, sliding them both under the covers and draping his arm over her shoulders so she'd fit herself to his side.

"How did things go today with Alexandra?"

He clenched his teeth just for a second. Okay, so subconsciously he'd still been hoping for *I love you. Make me yours forever.*

"Good, actually. I was an ass to her when she came to visit me in Nebraska."

"Why?" She raised up on her side.

"Good question." He reached to stroke her hair. "I think I was a different person then. Sounds nuts that someone can change in a few short weeks, but I think I have."

She frowned. "How?"

He stopped stroking, his hand still in her hair while he struggled to form his answer. "The idea of family. Of being part of some body of people who need connection to you. The idea of being responsible to anyone but myself. Those were missing for me."

"And now they're not?"

"No." He tried to keep the tenderness out of his gaze but he was pretty sure he couldn't. "Now they're not. Or they're a damn sight better, anyway."

She swallowed and looked away. He was making her nervous. She wasn't going to ask what had changed because she knew. And that knowledge made her nervous.

Okay. He could wait. He had time. He had all the time in—

His satellite phone rang out a summons, as if it was trying to make a liar out of him. He rolled halfway out of bed, grabbed his leather jacket off the floor and fumbled in the inner pocket, hoping it was Shana with new instructions for the next day's activities, hoping it wasn't a case that would take him away from this woman he loved.

"Brett Devlin here."

An unfamiliar male voice started speaking. Police. In Scottsbluff, Nebraska. A teenage boy was missing. Could he help?

Brett's heart closed down. He sat up in bed, grabbed the hotel notepad and pen, wrote down the information and promised to be back in town on the next flight.

"What was that?"

He glanced over to find Layla looking at him with alarm.

"That—" Brett flung the pad down on the dark wood night table "—was my life."

"You have to go." She traced the raised pattern on the bedspread with her index finger, intent on the design.

"Yes."

He wanted to kiss her, to pull her back in his arms, to tell her she meant more to him than anyone else in the world. But now was not the time, not after what she'd been through, and not with a young runaway who needed his help.

So he squeezed her knee under the bedspread and dialed the number of his longtime travel agent in Nebraska. She worked out of her home and was used to him calling at odd hours. He could fly out there tomorrow morning, help find the kid, and be back here to get his truck and see Layla again, spend more time with her, help her through the waiting and the anxiety.

He watched Layla while the phone rang at the other end. She was sitting on the bed, curled in on herself, tracing the damn bedspread, and his heart gave a huge lurch.

The answering machine came on; he left a message and punched off his phone.

"Layla, I have to leave tomorrow. I don't know when I'll be back. We need to talk about what's happening between us, what we want to happen."

Her eyes went wide; her face turned panicky and strained. Brett sighed, feeling the tension ratcheting up in him a thousand times more than it had been.

"Okay, I'll go first. This isn't the time or place or way I wanted to say this, but God knows what will happen or how long I'll be away."

She gathered her knees up to her chest and stared at the lump under the covers as if it was the most fascinating thing she'd ever seen.

He looked up at the ceiling, hating this vulnerable feeling, hating this place, this situation. Loving her. "I want to be able to find out what we can have between us, Layla. I've never felt this way about anybody. I know we haven't exactly gone the normal dating route, but we've gone through more than most couples ever do. I want to find some way we can be in each other's future."

She swallowed, a loud, convulsive gulp. "But what…were you thinking?"

He dared hope. This was better than, *What, are you crazy?* "I was thinking when this is all over, you and Phoebe might want to come to Nebraska for a visit. A long one."

"And…if things are good, you would want me to stay there?"

He blinked. Could it be this easy? "Yes."

"I can't."

He sucked in a breath as if he'd been punched in the stomach. "You can't."

"No." She turned tortured eyes on him. "I can't deal with the scrutiny, the crowds. I need to be on my mountain. It's my home. I belong there in ways I can't even begin to explain to you. I can't live with people."

"You could try."

"I did try. I'm here."

He held up both hands, fingers tense and spread. "This is hardly normal day-to-day life, Layla. You're going through hell here."

"Brett." She spoke very gently and carefully, as if to a spoiled child. "I know myself. I know what I want and what I need."

He stared at her for another few seconds, then went to pull on his clothes while she huddled miserably on the bed. He'd put himself out there, figuratively naked, and been rejected. He didn't need to be literally naked, as well.

"What about Phoebe? Is that the best place for her to grow up?" He tried not to sound angry and frustrated, but he didn't remotely succeed. She was throwing them away without even giving them a chance. "On top of a mountain with no one around? What kind of life is that for a kid?"

She flinched. "That's not your concern."

"Well, it should be yours."

Her eyes flashed and he held up his hand. He had to go; he didn't want ugly words left between them. "Okay. I'm sorry. I don't want to fight. You're right. I overstepped. She's not my concern."

He finished buttoning his shirt and started on the cuffs. "Have you given this some thought? I mean, about us? Or is this a knee-jerk reaction?"

"I've thought about it, Brett." She hugged her knees tighter. "A lot. I do…care for you. But this is my decision. I didn't make it lightly."

"So this is it." He gestured and let his arms slap down to his sides. "I leave tomorrow and it's good-bye?"

Her face turned to stone; her eyes were glassy and fixed. "Is there any other way?"

"No." He pulled on his jacket, bitter now and growing furious, frustrated. He wanted to shake her, wanted time to show her how wrong she was, even knowing it wouldn't do him a damn bit of good. "Not if your mind is made up."

"It is." She whispered the words, as if she could barely produce a sound.

"Okay then." He nodded, hands on his hips.

"Well, it's been an adventure, Layla. One I don't think I could have had with anyone else."

He gritted his teeth at the sight of her miserable face, resisted the impulse to kiss her one more time, and walked out of the door.

CHAPTER FIFTEEN

LAYLA WOKE to the mid-December darkness in her cabin and hugged her grandmother's quilt up to her chin, trying to savor the peace and utter relaxation, bracing herself for the sharp ache of pain that always interfered. She'd woken up on her own in this cabin every morning, day in and day out for eight years, and only once with Brett beside her in the bed. But the memory of that one morning had been deeply branded onto her waking consciousness and she had yet to find a way to heal.

She took a deep breath and let it out. Give it more time. She'd only been home a couple of weeks. She couldn't expect to get over him that quickly. Granted, she'd been surprised at how much he'd intruded into her daily routines, but that would change. He'd gradually fade from her memories as her life moved forward.

Phoebe wasn't yet awake, but judging by the feel of the morning, she would be soon. At three and a half months, she was settling into a more predictable routine. Amazing how different two little people could be. Where Alycia had been unflappable, calm, adaptive, Phoebe was feisty and demanding. Layla had a much harder time putting her down and going about her own business.

And she had to say, she loved it. Of course, her

pottery business was going to hell, and her cabin looked as though a fraternity had held a hazing party there, but interacting with this little carbon copy of herself had been an incredible experience.

She was convinced, though, that something had changed. It wasn't just that she'd bonded with her own flesh and blood because Phoebe was her birth daughter. Layla had changed. Something had opened her heart where it had been closed before. And there wasn't any great mystery what that something had been.

For another moment, before she got out of bed, lit a fire, started on the day's chores, she let herself remember their time together in Seattle, in her hotel room the night before he'd left. When Brett had been talking about Alexandra, and how he hadn't wanted anything to do with her until something had changed him.

That same something had changed her.

They weren't meant to live their lives together, but they had done something important and lasting for each other that she'd be willing to bet no one else could have. She'd brought him to his family, and he'd brought her the ability to be a good, loving mom.

After he'd left, she hadn't shut herself off the way she usually did. She'd allowed herself to grieve—she was still allowing herself—and had said yes, often, when Shana invited her to stay for dinner or overnight after Layla's daily visit to Phoebe.

Brett's sister hadn't said much, but it was clear from the bit she'd let slip now and then—by the way she kept Layla apprised of every phone call from Brett, by the way she insisted Layla take Brett's satellite phone number back with her—that Shana thought the two of them were making a colossal mistake and she fully expected one or the other of them to recognize it soon.

But Shana didn't understand. Beyond the fact that Keith was the love of her life, he fit with Shana; they would make a wonderful life together with minimal effort. Brett would go out of his mind living in this cabin and Layla would go out of hers living in his populated world. Love wasn't enough for them.

She was thrilled to be back, to be settled. To have her own things and her own food—though she did vary her menus a lot more now. Thrilled to be away from the intense emotions and the pain she encountered daily in Seattle. Not to mention the constant barrage of people, including reporters hungry for her and Phoebe's story—though Bruce had been wonderful keeping their interference to a minimum. By the time she'd walked away from Alycia, whom she'd weaned gradually over her weeks there, it had been almost a relief, after all the anticipation, to just get to the pain of separation and start working through it.

Layla thought of Alycia every day, missed her every day. Promised herself she wouldn't lose touch with her other little girl. And she knew she wouldn't. She wrote her a postcard every week. Drew her a picture sometimes or sent her a little mug or plate she'd made or toy she picked up in Leavenworth.

She went there more frequently now. It didn't seem so daunting a place after managing Seattle for so long. And it was nice to be in the pottery shop, to see Alice, the manager, and to interact with customers occasionally. She also got a lot more strawberry milkshakes at the Corner Creamery, which made the trips even more worthwhile.

A burst of baby outrage let Phoebe's mother know

in no uncertain terms that it was time for breakfast. Layla grinned and got out of bed, picked Phoebe up for a kiss and carried the baby over to the woodstove to show her how to make a fire.

Which, obviously, in Phoebe's estimation, took forever.

"Hey, there, little one, screaming won't make it go any faster."

Phoebe stopped screaming and stared at her mother solemnly as if she had spoken words of enormous importance.

"I'm serious." Layla stuck out her tongue and wiggled it around. "I'm totally serious."

Phoebe gave a shriek of laughter and bopped Layla on the cheek. Layla captured her hand and pretended to eat it, which made Phoebe laugh even more.

Layla laughed back—it was impossible not to—and winced at the usual stab of pain. If Brett were here, they could all three be laughing together.

She felt the tears coming yet again. When would she be rid of this grief? When would she be able to recover from this man's invasion into her heart and be able to move forward? She missed him. She missed his presence, his conversation, his humor, his body, his smell, his taste, his arrogance, his…everything.

She'd thought of calling him when she was in Leavenworth. She'd taken the number Shana had given her and stared at it for a full five minutes. What was the point? What would she say?

Nothing had changed. They'd known each other less than a week, for heaven's sake. And during that week they'd been immersed in an intensely dramatic, emotional situation. That kind of situation could inflame passions that wouldn't have been inflamed in everyday interactions.

Maybe Brett already regretted going overboard. Back in his own life, he probably barely thought of her. The whole episode must seem a distant, dramatic dream to him. Damn shame it didn't to her.

She closed the glass door of the stove on the crackling fire, carried Phoebe over to her rocker, sat the eager baby in her lap and brought out her breast. Phoebe latched on right away and began sucking vigorously. She'd taken to nursing after only a few anxious days where she and Layla had gone head to head over the concept. But Phoebe had proven herself strong and adaptable, like her mom. Built for the tough life ahead of her.

Layla stroked the soft cheek, captured the tiny hand grabbing painfully at her skin, and spoke gentle words of love and encouragement.

Was this the life she wanted for her child?

She stopped herself before all the doubts and questions went on and on, over and over, as they'd been going on and on, over and over for the past month and a half.

What was the point? She wanted to be here; she wanted to be with Brett. She wanted this life for herself and her child; she wanted Phoebe to have a different one.

Right now it was beyond her to sort out. But like that morning she'd gone into school, seen Phoebe's namesake and known her life would be different from her parents', different from her peers, like that afternoon she'd come home and found her parents dead and known she'd live away from people, she had a feeling someday, maybe even someday soon, something would happen to make everything clear.

BRETT SEARCHED THROUGH his refrigerator for anything that looked edible and dinner-worthy. Damn tough string of cases. He hadn't been home for more than two nights in a month. His truck was still out in Seattle; he'd been driving a rental car and hadn't yet found two free days to fly out and drive it back. Tomorrow, he promised himself, or the next day.

He popped open a beer and took out a carton of eggs in disgust. Another omelet made with wilted vegetables. But last time he'd eaten at Ida's Good Times Café, he'd been up all night in a vain attempt at digestion.

Hell, he'd been sleeping like crap for weeks. Not like him. Not that it was any mystery why. He couldn't get the damn woman off his mind for more than the little bursts of intense concentration needed for his work. He was thankful for the hectic pace of the last weeks, thankful not to have more time to think about her, wonder about her, worry about her. Was she doing okay with Phoebe? Were they getting along? Did she miss him? Had she reconsidered?

God, he wished she had a phone. He'd called Shana about a million times during the custody process, wanting news, which Shana dutifully supplied without his having to ask. He'd told her his own news, sure she'd pass it along to Layla in her own brand of supportive sisterly matchmaking. But he wanted to talk to Layla himself.

He broke three eggs into a bowl and mixed them viciously with a fork. Yeah, he wanted to talk to her. But he only wanted to talk to her if she was going to say she'd come to her senses. That she loved him. That she couldn't live without him. That she wanted to find some way, *any* way, to make it work.

Otherwise, what was the point? What was the damn point of renewing the connection, of pulling all those feelings and longings that he'd managed to dull only slightly in the past weeks out to the forefront again, and have to start at square one with the pain if she stuck to her stubborn-ass determination to be a hermit?

He chopped an onion and a red pepper, sautéed them in butter in his omelet pan. Was she still eating porridge, peanut butter and pasta? P-foods? Or had she allowed a few other letters into her menu? Did she think of him when she sat in front of the fire at night? Did she want to tell him when Phoebe did something new, something amazing?

He poured the eggs into the pan and shook his head to try and fling her out of his thoughts. What the hell was he supposed to do with all this emotion? Just stand here, cooking his omelet by himself, and plan to spend the rest of his life getting over her?

Two words: screw that.

He pulled his phone out of his pocket and dialed his sister, who answered on the second ring.

"Shana, Brett."

"Brett! Where are you?"

He could hear Alycia squawking in the background. She was in Shana's care until the adoption came through, apparently any day now. "I'm home. I need to come and get my truck."

"Of course, it's here. Keith keeps wanting to drive it and play cowboy detective like his future brother-in-law, but I won't let him."

Brett chuckled. "He can if he wants. I'll try to fly out tomorrow."

"Okay."

He waited. He knew that way of saying "okay" meant that she had something else on her mind and he only needed to wait until she made it sound as if it had occurred to her spontaneously.

"So…"

Five…four…three…two…one…

"Are you going to drive straight back home?"

He clenched his jaw and wandered out of the kitchen into his living room. "Yes."

"Brett! The two of you are complete idiots."

"Why, thank you."

Shana gave a long-suffering sigh. "I was betting on you to come to your senses first."

Brett rolled his eyes. "Yeah, well, don't bet too much. I came to my senses, as you call it, once before, and was sent packing."

"Oh, Brett."

"Apparently I don't compare well to mountain-tops." He was appalled at the sulky bitterness in his voice. Was that how he'd end his days? In the throes of a glorious lifelong pity party?

"Hmm." He could practically hear her brain spinning to find encouragement. "But she's been alone up there for these past couple of weeks, after being around us for so long, and hearing about you. I'm sure she's missing you, Brett. You should have seen how her eyes lit up every time I said you had called, even though she tried to pretend that she wasn't thrilled."

He took a deep breath. "She has to see that she can make it here. She still has this idea that people look down on her or something. I don't know what it is.

But the next move has to come from her. If I show up there when she's not ready, not expecting me, nothing resolved, the only thing that will happen is panic. I know it. I know her.''

"Brett. She loves you. You have to try."

"I know she does. That's the frustrating—'' Brett wrinkled his nose. The omelet. "Gotta go. Burning dinner. I'll be out there tomorrow or the next day."

He clicked off the phone and ran into the kitchen, turned off the stove and instinctively grabbed the pan off the burner. *"Ow. Damn."*

He slammed on the faucet and held his burned fingers under the cold water until he was sure the burning process was finished. Then he dared a peek. Blistered. Nasty. He had cream somewhere.

Somewhere…

He went to the closet outside the bathroom where he kept sheets, towels, extra soap and razor blades, medicines and other supplies. Rummaged around. Not on that shelf. Why the hell not? He knew he had it.

He stood on tiptoe, feeling around on the highest shelf. His hand closed over a box; something clicked in his memory, an eerie thrill of anticipation. He withdrew the box and opened the lid.

Day after day, week after week, with stubborn, unreasonable persistence, he'd gone after what he wanted. And here was proof that he could succeed.

His grandfather's watch.

LAYLA SMILED at Mrs. Brody at the Corner Creamery and accepted her strawberry milkshake, took her first wonderful, soothing sip, sitting at the counter with Phoebe on her lap. Her new measure of how wonderful something was: she could almost forget about Brett when she was drinking one of these.

Almost. It was just too easy to imagine him next to her, drinking one himself.

If he even liked them. Who knew? It seemed impossible they'd been together such a short time. She had to remember that, as deeply as she felt about him, she barely knew him.

Phoebe reached for the milkshake straw, nearly upsetting the entire glass. Layla laughed and held it out of reach. ''You have to wait a while yet, Ms. Grab-it-all.''

''A-dah.'' Phoebe made her pronouncement with all the official wisdom of a queen.

Layla hugged her tiny body close. The shop felt warm, cozy and festive, decorated for Christmas, though not very crowded in this chilly weather. Mrs. Brody could even pass for Mrs. Claus in her red sweater and white-haired, red-cheeked, wrinkly cheer.

Layla had had an unusually good afternoon in town today. Alice Cranston, the pottery shop manager, had commented on how happy and well she looked; a customer had shocked the hell out of her by admiring her talent out loud, saying she had a whole dinnerware set designed by Layla, and she'd actually been nervous meeting her. As if Layla were some sort of celebrity. Even higher on the shock-o-meter, Alice said that wasn't unusual. A lot of people asked after her, wanting to know something about the mysterious person who made the beautiful pottery they loved.

Layla took another sip of her milkshake, nursing the warm glow she still felt. It was almost as if someone else had taken over her body. As if these people were talking about an alien clone who'd been in town impersonating her, charming and intriguing all these strangers.

Because it was too weird to think it was her.

Phoebe made another of her emphatic pronouncements and Mrs. Brody beamed. "Your daughter is a darling. I'm so glad you've decided to share her with us a bit more often."

Layla took another sip to mask her embarrassment. "Thank you."

"She's so sweet. How old?"

"Three and a half months."

"Looks just like you."

"Yes." Layla couldn't help her proud smile. She loved it when people noticed.

"Well, you should bring her around more." She leaned confidentially on the counter, a pose that usually got Layla's guard up. Instead, Layla took another sip of her drink, eyebrows raised to show she was listening. "I've worried about you."

Layla hadn't a clue what to say to that. *Worried* about her?

"Young lovely thing like you up there by yourself. Whatever possessed you? Must be horribly lonely on top of that mountain."

Layla shrugged. "I like being alone."

The accustomed phrase was automatic, but for some reason the words rang strangely in her ears, sounded wrong the way she said them.

Yes, she liked being alone. But here she was, seeking company and enjoying it more than once a month. This was her third trip in December. She found herself restless way too often, even with Phoebe for company, wanting something...or someone.

Mrs. Brody pursed her lips. "Seems to me you

ought to be finding a young man to help you up there.''

But Brett wouldn't like living here. He'd made it clear the move was hers to make—to Nebraska. Over the last eight years she'd found her way, established a life for herself all by herself, proved that she could do it.

But could she do that elsewhere? Could she be accepted in other places, or was this some kind of freakish luck?

She thought of Shana and Keith, Anne and Bruce. She almost missed them. She sometimes wanted to call Shana to chat, and not just for news of her brother. And she often lingered on the phone after she'd carried on a one-sided conversation with Alycia when the baby was in the mood.

Brett's face rose up in front of her, the way he'd looked that day she told him why she'd gone up north to Glacier to have her baby. *I just hope someday you'll run to people when you need them, instead of away.*

And she suddenly knew exactly what she'd do with the number Shana had given her.

CHAPTER SIXTEEN

LAYLA SAT ROCKING in her chair, feeding Phoebe, feeling drained and lifeless and ready for bed, even though it was only just eight. She'd worked up all that energy to call Brett. Had been so sure of him, so sure of herself and what she wanted. She'd dug his number out of her bag and practically run back to the pottery store, where she generally made her calls. She'd even handed Phoebe to the startled Alice, since there were no customers in the shop, and bolted back to the office, closing the door behind her.

It had taken her two or three tries, but she'd finally worked up her nerve, worked out what she wanted to say, given herself every hope that he'd respond the way she dreamed of, that he'd invite her to visit, to give him and Nebraska, and people in general, a chance.

His voice mail had come on and she'd had to leave a message. A clumsy stammering message. "Hi, this is Layla. I want to come visit. Call me back." She'd rattled off the shop number, hung up and dropped her face in her hands. *I want to visit. Call me back?* Jeez. If he had any doubts about her ability to function in normal society, she'd probably cemented them right there.

Layla shifted Phoebe in her arms and managed to smile down at her sleepy face. Okay, so she stunk at leaving messages. For some reason it never occurred to her that he wouldn't be there, just waiting to take her call. Or that he wouldn't call back immediately.

He hadn't. She'd waited two hours in the shop, pacing the office, grabbing Phoebe back from Alice and pacing some more, showing her daughter her own work, other artists' work, explaining the process—as if she hadn't a dozen times already.

Finally, Phoebe had made it clear that pacing up and down a small pottery shop floor was not a three-month-old's idea of heaven. Or even close.

Layla had reluctantly settled her in the car with her groceries and driven back up the mountain.

Now she couldn't stand not knowing. Would he call and leave a message with Alice? Or wouldn't he call at all? She could go back down tomorrow, but the drive took a lot out of her, and if he hadn't called, the trip would be a waste of energy.

Except she was starting to think that staying up here not knowing would take a hell of a lot more out of her.

He'd call, wouldn't he? What if he didn't?

She made a sound of exasperation. Listen to herself. She sounded like a junior high student freaking out over her first crush. Only this was no crush. This was the real thing. And Layla had decided to give it a chance. If he called, if they decided to try, if they then crashed and burned, so be it. But if she didn't do this now, if she didn't at least try, she'd spend the rest of her days wondering if she'd made the biggest mistake of her life.

If he didn't call, there was her answer. She'd be no worse off than she was now—except that she'd be without hope.

The wind picked up outside and gusted against the shingled walls of the cabin. Another storm was predicted for tonight, though not nearly as bad as the one that had brought Brett to her.

Layla sighed. With her luck, it would be too snowy to drive down to the pottery shop tomorrow to check for messages, and she'd have to wait forever.

She closed her eyes, trying to relax, concentrating on the heavier and heavier feel of her daughter in her lap as the little body slowly gave in to sleep.

Five minutes later Phoebe had surrendered completely; Layla picked her up gently and brought her over to her crib, laid her in it, covered her with a blanket and bent to stroke her warm back and listen to her breathing, a fast, peaceful baby sound.

Then another sound. Layla's back went rigid. She shot up to standing, ears straining, eyes wide. What was that? The wind? A tree branch?

Another sound. A door? Who the hell was here? Her heart started pounding. Had Alice driven up to tell her she had a message? Had Brett called? Who was here?

She moved to the door and peered out, bending slightly to grab Jake. The snow was already falling, not terribly hard, but enough to obscure the view. A truck. Parked far from the house. Too dark to tell the make or color. No sign of the occupant.

Damn. *Damn.* Who the hell would park here and not come up to the house?

She grasped Jake more firmly, went to the front door, pulled her parka on, put her hand on the knob and counted, bracing her body for action.

One…two…three.

She flung open the door, leaped out into the chill and pulled Jake horizontal, her finger on the trigger.

A noise by the outhouse; she peered over, centered her weight between her feet. *Steady. Steady.*

The outhouse door opened; the dark shadow of a male figure emerged and began walking toward her.

"Stop." She made her voice loud and authoritative, and aimed where men hated to be aimed at.

The man stopped in his tracks; his hands went up.

"Move and I'll shoot. I'm aiming south of your navel and I don't miss."

A slight sound reached her ears. What the hell was that? Was he mumbling to himself? It almost sounded like laughter. If he was laughing, he had a majorly sick sense of humor.

"Who are you?" Layla squinted through the snow. Why the hell didn't he *say* something? "What do you want?"

"You, Layla."

Layla gasped. *"Brett."*

"Yes, ma'am. Having a little déjà vu moment here."

"Brett." She gave a bizarre hiccup of laughter and lowered Jake. He was here. *He was here.* That had to be good. That had to mean—

"No offense, but if you want more kids, you're going to have to stop trying to shoot me in that particular spot."

The male shape started walking toward her through the snow, his movements endearingly familiar. Then his face and form materialized out of the darkness and her heart couldn't decide whether to speed up impossibly faster or to stop altogether. God, he was gorgeous. And she was—

His previous words suddenly made it through to her chaotic brain. "Did you say more kids?"

"Don't you want more?"

She laughed again, uncertain what to think, what to feel, whether he was serious, whether she should answer. "I don't...I mean...I do. That is—"

He chuckled and opened his arms. "Come here. I missed you like hell."

She ran the remaining few steps. He caught her, one arm around her waist, one across her shoulders, and held her so tightly she could barely breathe.

She didn't care. Who needed air?

They stood together, Layla wrapped in his arms, her chest heaving with dry, joyous sobs, his warm, familiar scent against her cheek. He was here. He was here. She was holding on to him and could still scarcely believe it.

He released her, only to gather her back in and kiss her. She responded with her whole heart, almost unable to grasp that she was feeling him, tasting him, everything she'd been so afraid she'd only be able to do in fantasy for the rest of her life.

Finally he pulled back and grinned at her, brushing her hair away from her face, moving his thumb across her lip, touching her cheek, as if he couldn't get enough of the feel of her.

"Did you get my message?" She curled her fingers around his wrists and, brought them to rest on her shoulders, his hands cupping her face.

"Yes. I was dying to call back, but I was driving like hell and didn't want to stop. Or spoil the surprise." He glanced heavenward and blew out a breath. "I admit it was a lot easier showing up being sure of my reception."

Layla turned her head and kissed the inside of his wrist. "You thought I might send you away?"

"I wasn't going to let you do it easily, but yeah, I was afraid you would."

She lowered her head, stared down at their feet, dark shapes against the accumulating blanket of white. "I'm not ever going to be Ms. Sociability, Brett. I'm happier here than anywhere I've ever lived. But I'm done running from people I need, and I need to have a life with you and Phoebe."

He pulled her to him, kissed her forehead. "Come to Nebraska. Stay awhile and see. If you and Phoebe like it, we can buy a farmhouse together. Middle of nowhere, but enough people around that Phoebe can have school and friends. And we can spend summers here."

She nodded joyously. She wouldn't let fear win. Not this time. "It's what I want, too."

"Layla." He whispered her name, holding her too tightly, the vulnerability visible in his strong masculine face, even in the shadows. "I love you."

The words took her breath away. Maybe it was just that it was the first time she'd heard them. But she simply couldn't breathe, could barely think. He loved her. Real love. The kind that stuck around. It made her so happy, but in a strange, panicky kind of way that froze her. She had to say it back. She knew it was true. He was waiting. She had to—

"Let's go in. It's cold, and I'm dying to see how Phoebe's grown." He turned her gently toward the cabin, once again understanding her mood, that she wasn't quite ready, giving her the gift of a transition back to their normal, easy way together.

She took two steps ahead of him toward the cabin and turned back. "I love you, too, Brett."

Her voice came out thin, wavery and determined in the dark woods.

She heard his breath go in, then he lunged forward and caught her, squealing, up in his arms and carried her the rest of the way into the cabin.

Inside, he gently put her down, kissed her with love and passion so that she wanted to cry and dance around, but also hold still and be solemn. He was here, and when he left, she'd be leaving with him.

They walked together toward the crib and looked down at Phoebe, sleeping soundly; blond curls mussy, cheeks flushed pink. More babies, he'd said. Babies that would look like him and her. The two of them.

She gazed around at all her beloved familiar things, at the cabin that had been her safety for so long. She thought about it while they stood there, hands resting together on the crib railing.

That's what the cabin, her mountain, her isolation, had been all these years. Her safety.

But wherever Brett was—here or Nebraska or anywhere else in the world—that was her home.

EPILOGUE

BRETT PULLED the Cherokee up to Keith's town house in Seattle.

Layla stared out the window at the familiar building and smiled. Here she was again, arriving at the house in her Cherokee with Brett driving and a baby in the back. But so much had changed. Chilly gray November had given way to flowery green June, Phoebe was now nine months old, pulling herself up to stand, showing all too much of her mom's fierce independent streak. Layla called Nebraska home, though she'd never sell the cabin. In fact, the three of them were going to spend the summer on top of her beloved mountain—barring any emergency calls for Brett—after Alexandra's wedding weekend here in Seattle.

She looked down at the exquisite sapphire-and-diamond, channel-set ring on her left hand, turned it around and around with her thumb. And instead of being on their way to splitting up forever, she and Brett were going to be married.

"Hey."

She turned and smiled into the eyes of the man she adored. "Hey what?"

"A little déjà vu?"

She laughed. "Sort of. Except everything's so different."

He leaned forward for a warm kiss. "Mmm. Not everything."

"Ah-*da.*" The indignant baby shriek made them both jump.

"Okay, okay." Brett reached back and tickled Phoebe, who burst into her deep baby chortle. "Let's go."

Layla got out of the car. The door to the town house burst open and Shana emerged, followed by Anne Lehr, holding baby Alycia.

Layla's heart did a triple jump. She sped up the walk, greeted the two women warmly and gazed at the baby she'd raised for the first two months of her life. "She's so huge! She's so beautiful!"

Alycia reached out a hand and grabbed onto Layla's offered finger. "Ga-bum."

Anne beamed and traced a loving hand over the wispy blond hair. "She's a wonderful child. She's made us so happy."

"Oh, look!" Shana rushed down the walk and clasped her hands together, leaning over the car seat Brett was carrying. "Hello, little girl."

Phoebe frowned. Layla held her breath. *Come on, Phoebe, smile for Aunt Shana.*

The little face cleared and Phoebe let loose a torrent of welcoming baby babble.

"Don't *I* get a hug?"

Shana laughed and threw her arms around her brother. "You're just not as cute as she is. Can I hold her?"

Brett sent Layla a questioning glance. Layla nodded. "Of course."

Shana picked Phoebe up and held her reverently, then brought her up the walk to meet Alycia. The babies stared at each other in fascination. "You'll probably never know the whole story," Shana said quietly, "but you little girls have a lot in common. I hope you'll be friends for your whole lives."

Layla watched Anne and Shana, their faces somber, as was her own. No doubt they were all thinking back on the past year, the hopes and struggles and loss and adjustments. Shana's last words rang in her head. *I hope you'll be friends for your whole lives.*

She cleared her throat, uncomfortable still with expressing emotion, but full of how right and important it was to say, "I hope we all will be."

Anne and Shana looked up from the enthralled baby girls, eyes bright, smiles wide. If they were surprised at the sentiment coming from Mountain Girl, they didn't show it.

"What's going on out here?"

Three beautiful, elegant women—one redhead, one blonde and one brunette—emerged from the house and broke into the bonding moment before it became awkward.

Brett had told her the trio would probably be here. One of them must be Alexandra—the redhead. The other two were probably her best friends—Katherine, the tall brunette, and Hannah, the lovely blonde. The three of them had started Forrester Square Day Care, and in doing so had uncovered family tragedy, betrayal and loss, and from it all had created many happy beginnings.

Layla took a deep breath. She felt comfortable with Shana and Anne, but it still wasn't in her nature to love being swallowed up by groups—it never would be. She was a lot better than she'd been six months ago. Brett's love and acceptance had done wonders for her self-esteem. She'd worked through a lot of the feelings of betrayal and neglect and had managed to dredge up a healthy amount of love for her fellow man in the process. But still...

She proudly accepted the cooing over baby Phoebe, and held herself tall for the introductions, congratulating Alexandra on her upcoming wedding, noting the tremendous combined energy and warmth of the three women. Remarkable women. For one second, she felt small and dull in comparison.

A strong male arm wrapped around her waist; a male mouth nuzzled her ear. "Have I ever told you how amazing I think you are?"

She turned and laughed up at Brett, all awkwardness gone from the strength of his love for her. He could sense every nuance of every emotion she was feeling. "I think once or twice."

"Come in, come in. I—*Layla!*" Shana lunged and grabbed Layla's left hand. "What is *this?*"

Brett laughed. "That didn't take you long."

Layla glanced apprehensively at Alexandra. Some brides didn't care for having any of their thunder stolen. "I hope you don't mind. It's your weekend. I thought we should wait, but Brett—"

"Nonsense." Alexandra gazed at her stepbrother with obvious affection. "He's right to be proud. Many congratulations to both of you."

"This is the weekend for good news!" Shana gestured to the tall, beaming brunette beside her. "Katherine, tell them."

"I'm going to have another daughter." Katherine put her hand protectively over her barely bulging abdomen. "My father is beside himself. Did you ever meet him, Brett? Louis Kinard?"

Brett shook his head. "I heard his story from Shana, though. Not pretty."

Layla smiled her congratulations to Katherine. Brett had told her that Olivia Richards—Hannah's mother, and the woman who'd tried to ruin Louis Kinard's life—was going to trial the following month and was guaranteed a lengthy sentence.

Katherine shrugged, as if the gesture erased the importance of everything that had gone before. "It's all behind us now. Dad loves his new career consulting for the airline industry. But I really think he was born to be a grandfather. He spoils my kids like mad."

Hannah squeezed her friend's shoulder. "That's what grandparents are for."

"Let's go in." Shana opened the door to herd everyone inside. "I have coffee and extremely caloric pastries to start the weekend off right."

She went into the house, Brett, Anne and Alycia following, then Layla.

The rest of the group proceeded toward the kitchen. For some reason, Layla turned back.

The three women who were strangers to her, Katherine, Alexandra and Hannah, had stayed out on the stoop, standing quietly in the bright June sunshine. As if from some silent signal, the three of them moved closer together and draped their arms across each other's shoulders.

Layla took in a breath and held it. The picture of the three women captured her. Their friendship, the stories she'd heard about the trials they'd gone through, alone and together. The love between them, the power of their personalities. Three distinct individuals, one blonde, one brunette, one redhead, united together by love and history and by the good they'd accomplished for themselves and so many who came into contact with them.

She thought of the piece she'd made for Alexandra and Ben's wedding present. A platter in blues and greens, capturing some of the pattern of the wedding ring quilt her grandmother had left her. Maybe she'd do another piece, something for the day-care center— a piece celebrating these three beautiful women and the power of their friendship.

The women turned back, as if they caught the current of her thoughts. She started to look away, embarrassed to be caught staring, when she realized they were pulling her in, too. With their smiles, their warmth.

Instead of withdrawing, she smiled back. And it suddenly occurred to her that in the past year, she'd found much more than Brett, much more than home.

She'd found a family.

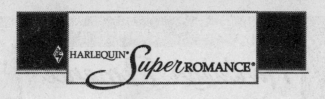
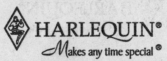